Shadow Blessed

The Shadow Accords 1

D.K. Holmberg

Shadow Blessed

ASH Publishing
dkholmberg.com

Chapter 1

The din of the street made it hard for Carth to follow the sounds of her mother's footsteps. Normally they made a sharp snap with each step of her heels along the cobbles, but today the sound was muted. Carth scurried forward, trying to catch up to her mother but only managed to grab onto the hem of her mother's dark green dress that blended in with the others around them.

Her mother looked down at her with her wide brown eyes and smiled. "Follow only, Carthenne." The words were an admonishment, one that Carth deserved. The game was to follow her mother until she could no longer track her, not tag along and hold on to her clothing, but something bothered Carth today, though she couldn't quite put a finger on what it might be.

She released her grip and stood still as her mother continued down the street. People passed around her, but Carth ignored them, keeping her gaze fixed on her mother's dress and the raven hair hanging in waves beyond her shoulders, hair that was not unlike her own, and listened.

1

The steady thudding with each step began to grow more distant but didn't disappear even after the sight of her mother faded completely. Only then did she start forward again, keeping her focus on what she could hear of her mother.

That was the trick of the game. Follow, but not so closely that her mother *knew* that she followed. If she could manage that, if she could trail her mother without her mother knowing she was there, Carth would win—at least that part of the game. The other part involved her father.

Where was he?

His part in the game was to follow Carth, but to do so unseen. This was a game they played often, one that her parents had started when she first managed to walk, and continued with each stop on their travels. Now twelve, she played the game well, but still not as well as her parents.

Focusing on the sound of her mother's footsteps, she continued after her, straining to hear them. The sound had grown faint, almost to the point where she couldn't be completely certain what she heard, but still she detected the rhythm she recognized as her mother's, one that even the noise on the street around her couldn't overwhelm.

Someone shoved her from behind and she spun, dancing back toward the wall behind her as her father had taught in another game. There were dozens of different games played, often at the same time. Over the years, her father had added new games, all while keeping her playing the older ones as well. Each game built on skills he taught her in the last, his way of passing time and helping her learn each city they stopped in, getting her comfortable regardless of where they ended up.

Nyaesh was no different. Perhaps more dangerous—the attacks she'd overheard her parents speak about outside the city made it seem different than what she had experienced in the last city—but the games continued.

Don't let me touch you.

She could almost hear his voice as he instructed her. She wasn't nearly as good at that game as she was with the following game. Carth looked for her father but didn't see him, only a man in a tattered black cloak who glared at her when she stared too long. He carried something under his arm, and as she watched, he stepped around a corner into an alley and disappeared.

Her father would still be following her, but where was he?

She backed against the wall, shifting her braided black hair over her shoulder while watching the street for signs of movement that were out of place. Her parents had taught her that trick, instructing her to pay attention at all times and concentrate on what seemed unusual. In the streets of Nyaesh, a place with a river running along one shore and the trade road passing by the other border, peoples from all over traveled, making it more difficult to pick out what seemed out of place. There were certain patterns that she'd learned to pay attention to, and types of clothing that she knew to be concerned by. Her parents always wore clothing that blended in rather than standing out, making it that much more difficult to find them.

Another man with a tattered cloak passed and Carth watched him from the shadows. Was that the same man who'd bumped into her? No… the height was wrong and this man had more sloped shoulders. He turned the same corner, though, and disappeared down the same alley.

Two men with heavy tattoos along their arms, colorful marks that ran from their wrists all the way to their exposed shoulders, passed her. One of them flicked his gaze to her and she shrunk even deeper into the shadows. These weren't streets for someone her age. That was why her parents played the game, and why her father watched from the shadows. They wanted her to learn safety and find a way to protect herself.

You don't have to be the largest if you're the smartest.

That was another of her father's lessons. There were countless of them, and they stuck—mostly because he said them often enough that they would.

Another group passed. The men wore headscarves and long, shimmery robes and made no effort to hide the curved swords at their sides. Most in Nyaesh hid their weapons, but the A'ras wore them openly. A sash of maroon so deep that it looked like dried blood was wrapped around one's upper arm, and another wore the sash looped through his robe. The maroon, much like the unseen tattoos on their hands, marked them as the royal protectors and servants of the faith, men with power that came not only from their mastery of the sword, but also from the magics they were able to use. Carth had never seen them use their power, but her parents had her watch them often enough to know to steer clear.

Most in Nyaesh did the same, moving out of the way so that the A'ras didn't come too close.

A man with arms bound in coils of rope struggled between them. Blood streamed from cuts on his neck, seeping beneath the black hood covering his face. Carth hurriedly looked away, already knowing his fate. Paying too close attention to the A'ras could prove dangerous to her anyway. As they passed, a shiver worked down her spine.

She felt the scuff of boots behind her and turned quickly, thinking that her father might have signaled his approach, but she saw only a haggard-looking beggar. Carth's nose turned up at the stench coming off him, and she backed away.

Where was her father?

Waiting here, she should have found him. That was the signal, a way of telling him that she struggled. He should have come to her by now. That he had not... either he thought the A'ras distracted her too much, or he didn't know that she wanted to end the game.

Carth glanced at the rooftops, but they were empty. The sharp slope would have been difficult to climb anyway, but it wouldn't have been the first time her father had traveled that way to hide from her. She stared at the shadows from intersecting alleys until they disappeared but saw nothing that indicated that he was there. Carth took a second glance at the people milling about in the street, thinking that he might have put on a different robe or wrap to hide his presence, but masking his height and muscular build would have been difficult.

5

She didn't see him.

This was the part of the game where she always struggled. She could track her mother by listening to the sound of her feet, or watching for the flash of color in her cloak, or the way she walked, or even the scent from the spices and herbs she'd been mixing, but she rarely managed to find her father when he trailed her. Her mother was good at the game, but her father was a master.

Carth realized that she'd spent too much time standing still, and that her father was not coming to her rescue. Maybe this was a new rule. She needed to follow her mother; only, where had her mother gone?

She scurried forward in the direction she'd last seen her, but she suspected her mother had turned a corner and disappeared down the street, fading into the people all around her. Carth wasn't tall enough to see over the crowd, and climbing would only draw attention to herself—another thing that her parents wanted her to avoid. Instead, she had to find another way to track. That was the reason that she'd grown so skilled at listening to the sound of her mother's feet, and watching for any sign of movement that would help her find her mother.

As she focused through the noise on the street, listening for her mother, other sounds drifted to her. Most were typical sounds of Nyaesh, those of hundreds of feet clomping on stones, or the soft and steady murmur of dozens of voices, even the occasional caw of a hawk soaring high overhead. Through those sounds, Carth heard an urgent murmuring, one that was unusual for this part of Nyaesh.

Moving more carefully, she searched for signs of her father, wishing that he would find her again. Usually they didn't let the game go on this long. What was different today? Unless they wanted to teach her something. Sometimes her father let her wander longer when he thought to demonstrate an aspect of the game that she hadn't mastered. Had grabbing onto her mother's dress too soon been a problem?

Near a small square, she paused at the low wall around its perimeter. The wall was only about four feet high, about the same as her, but smaller than the massive wall around the city. The market was held in the square in the mornings, but at this time of the day, the carts would be gone and the square empty.

Two people crouched over an unmoving figure sprawled along the street. They wore the long, shimmery robes and curved swords of the A'ras. One had a neatly trimmed beard, pointed at the chin and woven with gold. Carth knew that was a sign of rank, but not what it meant. The other was clean-shaven—a new member of the A'ras. Both wore a maroon sash.

A tall and slender third man wearing a long, dark cloak that was out of place even in Nyaesh stood off to the side, as if to avoid notice. His dress didn't mark him as A'ras and he didn't wear the maroon sash, either. A shiny scar ran along the edge of his face, behind his ear, working along the hairline. Something about this man made her uncomfortable.

Carth backed away. Gaining the attention of the A'ras

was a sure way to get hurt. That was one of the earliest lessons her father had taught her when they came to Nyaesh, and one that she had taken to heart. She didn't need her father to remind her to avoid those men and their wicked swords.

The slender man looked her way and she shrunk even farther back into the shadows.

She bumped into someone and spun quickly, wondering if her father had finally found her, but saw only another of the A'ras. He threw her away from him, sending her tumbling to the cold stone as he pushed his way past her, making his way toward the others.

"Did you find her?" Carth heard him ask as he approached.

Carth noted the slender man had deep green eyes that scanned the street. "We found her. Your men were too aggressive with her capture, Al-shad."

Carth had never heard one of the A'ras rebuked in such a way. They were feared, and for good reason. Even the Lasenguard, soldiers tasked with keeping peace in the countryside outside of the city, steered clear of the A'ras. That was partly because of their role with the royal family and partly because of their arcane skills. Yet this man spoke freely around them, and seemingly without fear of the deadly magicked blade of the swordmasters.

"My instructions were clear, Felyn." Al-shad stepped through the narrow opening into the clearing, moving away from the other man. He crouched and briefly stretched his hand toward the fallen figure before withdrawing it. Al-shad wiped his hand on his robe, a distasteful expression on his bearded face. "Fools," he snapped at the others. "She was to be taken alive. That was the agreement we made." He glanced at Felyn. "We needed answers."

Carth started forward and caught sight of the edge of green fabric.

Mother?

Her heart raced and she took an unintentional step forward.

Her mother couldn't be here, could she? She had known well enough to avoid the A'ras; she wouldn't have allowed herself to get so close that they harmed her, would she?

Where was her father?

Carth wanted nothing more than for the game to be over so she could return home. Her mother could continue teaching her about the herbs and spices of her homeland, and Carth would promise to listen better the next time, always more interested in learning from her father and the sly smile that he wore as he described ways to avoid detection.

A hand grabbed her wrist and she spun, hoping to see her father. Instead, an older man with pale blue eyes and a sharp nose looked past her. A heavy gray robe hung from his shoulders and he used this to wrap around her, backing them both deeper into the shadows.

"Let me—"

He clamped a hand over her mouth, squeezing so tightly that her eyes watered. "Quiet, girl."

She struggled to get free, fervently wishing for her father

to come to her rescue, but no one came. Men were known to abduct children in Nyaesh in spite of the A'ras patrols, such as they were, but the man seemed disinterested in her, ignoring her as he backed deeper into the shadows, looking beyond Carth toward the fallen woman.

Not her mother. Carth wouldn't believe that.

"She didn't say anything anyway," the bearded A'ras said.

"You gave her no chance," Felyn said.

The bearded A'ras glanced up the street. "You can obtain answers from him." He nodded to Al-shad. "That is, if you managed to capture him."

"Captured, yes, but he says nothing. We could have used them against each other. How long have they been here?"

"Long enough for me to notice," Felyn said. "Almost too long. If they were to succeed…"

Al-shad nodded. "We would have been discovered. A good thing you detected them."

Felyn sneered at him.

Carth attempted to free herself, but the man kept a tight grip over her mouth. Space had formed around the A'ras and the fallen person. She needed to get closer; she needed to know that it wasn't her mother lying on the cobbles.

"Unfortunately, with her gone we have no leverage," Al-shad said.

Felyn's gaze slipped up the street. The man holding Carth wrapped his cloak more tightly around her, shrinking back into the shadows. She struggled a moment, but as the slender man's gaze drifted over her, she actually prayed that she would remain hidden.

"More than you think. There is a girl," Felyn said.

"The woman was alone," the clean-shaven A'ras said.

"She had a girl," Felyn repeated. "She was the only reason I agreed to this fool plan. Find her."

The bearded A'ras reached for his sword. "You find her if she's so import—"

Felyn darted toward the bearded A'ras faster than Carth could track, catching him with a knife in his throat. When he stepped back, he kicked the clean-shaven A'ras hard enough that he crumpled next to the fallen woman, blood pooling around his side.

Al-shad reached for his sword, but Felyn moved faster, a narrow-bladed knife in his hand stabbing through Al-shad's before the man could unsheathe.

"Where is the man?" Felyn asked.

The clean-shaven A'ras jumped from the ground and darted toward Felyn, who barely turned and sliced with his knife, leaving the A'ras unmoving next to his companion. When he turned back to Al-shad, Carth noted a dangerous dark glint to his deep green eyes.

"The man. Where is he?"

"Baldun Temple. We wanted to draw out the Reshian threat. You will need me—"

"I have no need of you any longer, Al-shad." Felyn stabbed with the knife, sending it through his gut.

The A'ras grunted, and his hand slipped off the hilt of his sword. Al-shad coughed, a bubble of blood coming to his lips. "You will not leave the city alive, Felyn. You have violated the agreement…"

11

Felyn wiped his blade on Al-shad's robe as the man slipped to the ground before sheathing it once more. "I doubt you shared our 'agreement,' Al-shad. Other than you, who else will know? Besides, it means little to me."

As he turned to disappear down the street, Carth was pulled even farther into the shadows of the nearby building. For the first time, she didn't resist, letting the man keep her covered with his cloak. She didn't want Felyn noticing her, not with the ruthless way he'd killed—and so easily, especially considering the A'ras! When he walked past, a chill washed over her briefly before fading.

The man next to her stood motionless, holding his cloak around her. He didn't even seem to breathe.

After long moments, he pulled the cloak away and released his grip on Carth's mouth. "You would be wise not to scream."

She met his pale-eyed stare and could do nothing other than nod.

The man kept one hand locked around her wrist and dragged her forward, pulling her as he approached the three dead A'ras and the woman. Carth wanted to look away, but couldn't. She needed to know.

As she neared, she recognized stitching along the dark green fabric first, placed there by her mother years ago. She didn't need to see the waves of raven hair now strewn on the stone, or her mother's gentle lips, now unmoving, or even the silver ring on her finger to know that it was her.

Carth sobbed.

"Quiet," the man hissed.

Carth couldn't stop the tears. They dripped down her face and she wiped at them. Where was her father?

But even as she wondered, she knew. Al-shad had said there was a man at Baldun Temple, and there was the man she'd seen dragged through the street earlier. She hadn't been willing to look, but if she had, would she have recognized her father?

Why would the A'ras come for her parents?

"You know this woman?" The man knelt next to the A'ras and ran his free hand quickly over their bodies, dropping a pair of knives and a coin purse onto the ground next to him.

Was he nothing more than a scavenger? Had he *wanted* the A'ras to die so that he could search them?

When she didn't answer, he jerked on her arm again, forcing her to give him her attention.

"Girl! Do you know her?"

Carth stared at the silver ring on her mother's finger, woven to look like thorn branches pointing inward. Carth had never managed to pull the ring from her finger, and her mother never seemed to mind how the thorns poked her.

"She's my mother," she said in a whisper.

"Mother? And she managed to reach the city?" The man watched her a moment, waiting for Carth to answer, but there was nothing for her to say. He slipped the ring off her mother's hand and tossed it to Carth. "Best not to flash that around here, I think." Then he turned his attention back to the fallen A'ras.

Carth needed to get free. She didn't know what this man

13

might want with her, but her parents had warned her often enough what happened when adults attacked children. That was part of the reason they played the games with her. Once she got away, she could get to the temple and find her father. He needed to know what had happened.

And then what?

Carth's entire world had changed. Her mother was gone, not only killed by the A'ras, but because of that brutal man Felyn who had wanted her alive.

Which meant they wanted her father. Or worse—already had him.

She needed to find him, free him if she could. Then he might find a way to protect himself and her.

As the man moved on to the clean-shaven A'ras, Carth grabbed for one of the knives lying on the ground.

She did so quickly, spinning as she did and trying to pry her wrist free. Her father had shown her a few tricks, and she used one now, forcing her hand down while kicking at the same time.

The movement startled him, and she got free. Carth held the knife in front of her.

"That was foolish, girl," the man said. He kept his eyes on her face, ignoring the knife pointed at him.

Carth took a step back, unintentionally stepping into the square. That was a stupid move, and she knew it. The wall wasn't too high to climb, but high enough that it would slow her as she tried to escape. And she didn't think there were any other ways out of the clearing. Getting free would involve moving quickly.

"Come with me. I can keep you safe."

Carth shook her head, jabbing toward him with the knife. "My father will keep me safe."

"Your father is—"

She didn't wait for him to finish telling her what her father was.

Carth scrambled back and reached one of the walls. As the man approached, she reached for the top of the wall and pulled, throwing herself over the edge. She landed in a roll, already starting to come to her feet and darting toward the alley.

The man chased, leaping the wall with more agility than she would have expected someone of his age to be capable of.

The mouth of the alley opened before her, and she raced toward it. Like the one her parents played with her, this was a game, only this time, the stakes meant her life.

She ran, racing toward the temple, needing to find her father, but fearing that the slender assassin would have gotten there first.

Chapter 2

Carth lost track of how long she ran. Her sides ached and sweat left the entire back of her dress damp. She easily found where she needed to go. Most within the city knew how to find the temple, a place where men had once worshipped the god Baldun, but which was now empty. The temple rose near the middle of the city, higher than anything around it. She approached slowly, eyes drifting to the three towering spires of pale white stone that rose skyward before she pulled her gaze back to the temple itself.

She had never visited. Nyaesh had many areas that were unsafe and, according to her parents, the temple was one of the most dangerous places in the city. Now she approached alone and armed with only a knife stolen from a dead A'ras.

As she crouched in an alley, she paused to study the knife. It had a strange hilt of smooth black, with a texture like bone. The blade matched the hilt, nearly black as well. Carth had been careful not to touch the edge of the blade for fear of accidentally poisoning herself. Letters carved into the blade were in a language she didn't recognize.

Had a knife like this killed her mother? Had it been *this* knife?

Carth couldn't believe that her mother was gone. They had been playing a game, nothing more! Her mother would not have hurt anyone to deserve her fate.

Yet the A'ras and Felyn had sought her. They wanted her father. And they would have grabbed Carth if not for the *other* man trying to abduct her.

Had he been with them?

She'd lost him in the run from the square, but he had heard the same comment about the temple. If he'd followed her here, she didn't know if she could outrun him again. Her legs ached and her chest felt tight from the running.

Thinking of her mother brought tears to her eyes again, and she wiped them away. Father. She needed to find her father. Then she could mourn.

She focused her attention on the temple. A wide, arched door remained closed and no one moved along the street outside. Was that normal? She'd expected there to be more activity, especially after what she'd overheard.

After waiting for movement, Carth stepped away from the neighboring building and started toward the temple. She kept the knife at her side as she crossed the street, not wanting to draw attention to herself—but then, with the street empty, her presence alone would draw attention. She grabbed her braid and pulled on it, trying to calm herself. Her heart raced, but that could be as much from the run through the city as from nerves.

At the door to the temple, she pushed.

The door opened and she slipped inside. Lanterns hung on hooks along the walls, burning with a dull orange light, leading all the way down the hall.

Carth froze. She'd thought the temple empty.

A thick red carpet ran the length of the entry, leading toward a wide hall. The temple was supposed to be abandoned, her father having told her that the god Baldun had fallen out of favor. Though nothing moved in the distance, the lanterns made it clear that someone had been here.

What would she say if she was discovered? She had an A'ras knife, and if they learned that the others were dead, would she be blamed? Maybe she could find out why they had wanted her mother and why her father had been dragged to the temple.

She made her way carefully, watching for movement. With each step, she knew that she should turn around, but the possibility that her father was here, and that he was injured, pushed her forward.

What would she do if she came across any A'ras? She could run, but only so fast.

The carpet running the length of the hall ended, and she reached stone. Stepping forward, she made her way to the wall, not caring for how exposed she felt in the middle of the hall. A wide room opened in front of her, and the fading daylight streamed in through overhead windows. Carth paused but saw nothing in the room.

Where would they have taken her father?

And why did the temple seem empty?

She crept around the massive chamber, moving carefully. As she reached the opposite side of the room, a flash of movement caught her attention and she dropped to her stomach behind a tall pillar.

"They brought him here," a rough voice said.

Carth moved her head around the pillar, wanting to see but knowing that she should not. Anything that made her more visible put her in danger, but she needed to know.

"There's nothing here, Ander."

"I see that."

"Why the temple, though? Seems strange, especially since the Nyaesh abandoned the old god."

"As strange as how easily three A'ras died?"

"The A'ras have never been the threat they would like others to believe, Jhon."

"No," Ander said, "but that doesn't negate their skill. Dispatching three with the barest of movement... have you ever seen anything like it?"

"Not here," Ander whispered. "They shouldn't have reached here yet."

"You could have intervened."

"What would that have accomplished?"

"We might have someone to question," Jhon said.

The longer she listened, focusing as her parents had taught her when playing street games, the more she realized that she recognized one of the voices. Not Jhon. He had a youthful and deep voice, but not one that she'd heard before. Ander... that was the voice she recognized.

When she risked lifting her head, she understood why.

The older man who had tried abducting her stood beneath one of the lanterns on the other side of the temple. His gaze scanned the surroundings and Carth resisted the urge to throw herself further behind the pillar, but her father's warning voice told her to remain still. *Movement attracts attention. Stay at the edge of the shadows.*

When Ander's gaze turned away, she slowly moved back behind the pillar. Would they come over here as they searched the temple, or would she be safe remaining here?

"I thought we might find answers coming here," Ander said. "The Reshian…"

Jhon laughed softly. "You intended to intervene here, but not in the street?"

"That's not how it is done," Ander said.

"So you keep telling me."

"See what you can find. The A'ras claimed the other was brought here."

Footsteps thudded across the stone. Carth pulled her legs into her chest, trying to make herself as small as possible. If this man caught her, she doubted that she'd have the strength needed to escape.

As the footsteps came closer, she gripped the hilt of the knife tighter and slowly started to stretch her legs. If she needed to escape, she would be ready and would do whatever it took. Her father wasn't here. Carth hoped that he might have gotten back to their home and to safety.

"Anything?" Jhon's voice echoed across the emptiness.

The footsteps stopped. "There's nothing here."

"And not in the side rooms either," Jhon said.

"You've already checked them?"

"I don't need to open doors to know they're empty."

The footsteps thudded against the stone again, this time moving away. "Then we're leaving. Time to see what else we can learn."

"What of the girl?" Jhon asked.

"I'll find her soon enough."

Carth froze, careful not to move as the footsteps steadily made their way out of the temple. She almost refused to even breathe. Taking anything more than the shallowest of breaths risked exposing her. Her hand cramped from squeezing the knife.

Nothing more came through the temple.

Carth allowed herself to take a breath and slowly stand. Clinging to the pillar, she peered around it but saw nothing. As Jhon and Ander had reported, the temple was empty.

Her footsteps thundered in her ears as she made her way around the edge of the temple. Moving silently and without detection had all been part of the games she'd played with her parents. She'd never mastered it quite like her father. He could slip along behind her, making almost no noise, so silent that she would almost believe that he wasn't there. Carth had learned to find him by focusing on his breathing, and on the way the wind shifted when he did, touching her skin or pulling on her clothing differently.

Thinking of him made her throat feel thick again and she swallowed back the lump that formed. He *had* to be unharmed, didn't he? She couldn't believe that he would have been so easily captured, not knowing how well he could hide himself and how well he could keep hidden. So maybe the man she'd seen the A'ras carrying down the street *hadn't* been her father. If that was the case, she had to find him.

There was one place she could look, the place where they had agreed to meet in the event that they became separated. A place like that was necessary with their games, and they had wanted for her to have a place of safety, only she had never had to use it. Either they'd stayed close enough to her, or, as Carth had grown and become more skilled, she hadn't had the need. Until today.

Now she would go looking for her father only. Her mother would never join them again.

As she reached the hall and the transition from the tile to the carpet, Carth thought she saw movement at the edge of her vision. Had Ander or Jhon returned?

She should have been more careful. The temple was dangerous—she knew that—and she had relaxed her guard when she'd found it empty.

Carth ran.

With the first step, she realized that she should have remained still, or moved slowly at least. That had been the lesson her father had taught her. Sudden movement like this would only get her noticed, but her racing heart and fear for her father made her careless.

Was it her imagination, or did she hear footsteps?

She couldn't turn around. Doing so would only slow her. Instead, she gripped the knife tightly as she raced toward the door. Carth slammed her shoulder into it and went flying out of the temple to tumble down the steps outside.

Rolling to her feet, she hazarded a glance behind her.

There was movement inside the temple but she didn't remain long enough for them to catch her. If it wasn't Ander or Jhon, that meant it was one of the A'ras. Either way, she needed to move on. Her father wasn't here.

The empty street practically screamed at her presence as she ran. It wasn't until she managed to turn down a wider street leading toward the fortress at the heart of the city that people began to fill the streets. A few people glanced at her, but she hurried past, sneaking around them as she raced forward. Only after she made a few more turns did she finally allow herself to relax.

Carth knew most of the city well. That had been another of her parents' lessons. They hadn't been here long, but her mother had particularly wanted to ensure that she could find her way around without them. Most of the time, it didn't matter. When had she ever been left alone in the city before now?

She found the street market near the river. It was a busy place—a *public* place, and one that her father had instructed her to find if she ever needed them. Massive ships were moored along the docks of the Maladon River, so wide here as it flowed toward the sea. Most of the ships had markings, colors that she had long ago learned, but a few were unmarked.

Weaving through the crowd, Carth spied a pair of A'ras striding down the street. She shrunk away, back toward the shadows. What if they looked for her? Worse, what if Felyn came after them? The simple and brutal way he'd killed still left her with a chill. In Nyaesh, death was not an uncommon sight. It was the reason her parents feared for her as they did. But there were those who dealt in death much more publicly than others, and then there were men like Felyn, who seemed as if killing men mattered no more to him than catching and cleaning fish mattered to the sailors along the dock.

As she scanned the street, she saw another of the A'ras making his way up from the docks. Carth almost started forward, clutching the knife as she did. Anger surged in her over her mother, mixing with fear for her father and the helplessness that started to overwhelm her as she contemplated her next step—whatever that might be.

Two more of the A'ras appeared, and Carth shrunk back.

They stopped across the street, near enough that she could listen to their conversation, but as much as she might want to eavesdrop on the A'ras, she wanted to find her father more.

Carth crept along the wall, keeping her back hugging the stones as she slipped down the street. When she was far enough away, she hazarded a glance back. Nearly a dozen of the A'ras had gathered. One of them spoke rapidly, leaning toward the others as he did. They began to split off, with groups of them going in different directions down the street, each with swords unsheathed.

As a pair of the A'ras approached her, she hid behind a stack of boxes stinking of rotting fish until they were clear, feeling helpless. The A'ras were responsible for what had happened to her mother. Maybe not the ones she'd just seen—the men who had killed her were likely dead—but men like them.

She gripped the knife more tightly as she watched them. The A'ras thought nothing of killing, thought nothing of intimidation, and now her family had been caught up in it. Her mother was gone, probably her father too, though she hated to think that way, and she felt like she *had* to do something about that.

She might have a knife stolen from one of the dead A'ras, but what did she know about using it? What did she really think she could do if she was attacked?

What if she snuck up on them?

She could slip forward, slide the knife into one of their backs before they even knew she was there. Then she could run. Her parents had taught her to disappear and hide. She could blend into the street so that they never caught her.

But she still wouldn't have answers about why her parents were gone. Her father hadn't come for her. Didn't that mean he wouldn't? If he wasn't the man she'd seen captured, and if he remained free, why hadn't he found her by now?

The only reason was that he couldn't.

He was gone, like her mother.

Carth fought against tears, not wanting to break down. Not here, and not until she was safe, but where would she ever be safe again?

She had settled back into the shadows, tears welling in her eyes, when a hand grabbed her shoulder.

She spun, thrusting the knife out. An older man with soft

gray eyes caught her wrist and twisted it, forcing the knife away.

"Easy," he said. "You're the one hiding behind my catch."

Carth jerked her hand back, and he let it go. She held on to the knife but lowered it so that it wasn't pointing at him.

"What are you doing here?" the man asked.

Carth shook her head. The A'ras had disappeared along the street. Anything she might have thought about doing faded from her mind. "Nothing."

"Seems to me that a girl your age with a knife isn't doing 'nothing.' You going to tell me what you thought you might be up to, or do I have to notify the A'ras?"

She paled. "I didn't do anything."

The man shrugged. "Mayhap not, but they can throw you in the stocks until you answer."

Carth's eyes widened. "They wouldn't do that."

"You sure about that? Girl like you"—he motioned to her light blue dress, now stained from creeping about the city—"looks like you ain't never seen any real suffering. I think you might be surprised at what will happen until your parents come for you."

Carth started sobbing.

She tried controlling it, tried swallowing back the tears and the sadness and the fear, but she couldn't. Now that she had stopped, and now that no one seemed to be following her, it spilled from her.

"Aww, hey, now. I don't mean to upset you. Thought you might be one of the thieves sneaking off with my potatoes and dried fish." He stepped back and eyed Carth. "From the looks of you, that don't seem to be the case. Run along now to your folks and I'll leave you be."

As the man started to turn, Carth sobbed even more.

He paused and turned back to her. "What is it, girl?"

She tried stopping the tears, but failed. She took a step back and tripped over the hem of her dress, falling into a puddle of foul-smelling water that only made her cry more. Rather than moving, she wrapped her arms around her legs and cried.

When the man scooped her up, she didn't fight. And she didn't struggle when he carried her down the street. Her parents would have been disappointed. All the lessons they had tried to teach her disappeared in one burst of tears.

Chapter 3

A bell tinkled when the man pushed open a door, but Carth still didn't look up. The man hadn't carried her far, and she still had her knife. This close to him, she could stab him with it were she to need to, but the man didn't seem like he wanted to harm her.

The inside of the building he'd entered smelled of salt and meat and faintly of bread. Carth's stomach rumbled and she realized that she hadn't eaten since early in the morning, long before she'd seen her mother lying unmoving on the street.

At the thought of her mother, she started crying again.

"Hal, you don't be bringing any more strays in here."

Carth blinked at the sound of a woman's voice. Through the tears, she saw a wider woman with a long gray robe that brushed the floor. The woman held the long handle of a broom in her meaty fists, but her eyes were soft and warm and the frown on her mouth looked more gentle than angry.

"Not a stray, Vera. Found this girl outside the tavern. Thought she might be one of the damned thieves keep taking our supplies. Don't think that's the case at all. When I mentioned her parents, she got all weepy. Think she might be with the—"

"Shh," Vera said, slipping her arms underneath Carth and pulling her away from Hal. "You scared the girl!"

"Like I said, I thought she was one of the thieves."

"You don't know that there are thieves, Haldon Marchon! More likely, you just forgot to count the boxes right."

"I keep my inventory sheets straight. I can tell you whether anything is missing, and I know that there are crates that aren't accounted for."

"And you think this girl is able to drag away one of your crates?"

"Her?" Hal stood next to Vera and studied Carth. "Mayhap not, Vera. She's barely any bigger than the crates. I shouldn't have scared her like I did."

"I wasn't scared," Carth said softly.

"What did you say to her that got her all blubberin' like this? You can be sharp with your tongue, Hal!"

"You should talk. I said nothing except that I'd call the A'ras. Thought that might run her off more than anything. I didn't want to get her blubbering."

"The A'ras? You don't want the attention any more than she does, I don't think."

"That's not the point."

"Then what is? You think that lot can find anything, especially what with all the hassle they have keeping *them* in line?"

"Careful, Vera," Hal said in a whisper.

"They don't have ears in here. Tavern is empty, in case you haven't noticed."

"I know they haven't got ears in the tavern, but that's not the point."

Carth realized he was looking at her. "I wasn't scared," she said again.

Vera carried Carth to a chair and settled her into it. She reached for a steaming pot and poured spiced tea into a chipped ceramic mug. The paint along the rim had faded to a light pink. Carth wondered if it would have been almost maroon before, the same color as the sashes the A'ras wore.

The older woman took a seat on a bench wide enough to accommodate her girth and leaned forward until she was barely a hand away from Carth. "Don't let old Hal frighten you, girl. He talks mean, but he has a soft heart. Trust Vera on that."

Carth brushed her braid behind her head, watching Vera as she did. The old woman had gentle features and real warmth to her light blue eyes.

"Why do you still cry?" Vera asked. "I told you I won't let Hal harm you."

Carth shook her head. Even thinking of trying to answer made her throat swell. She didn't know these people. All she wanted was to find her father, but if her father had been safe, wouldn't he have come to the meeting place and found her? The fact that he hadn't made the alternative—that the A'ras had captured him—more likely.

She started sobbing again and wiped at her eyes with her fist, trying to dry them.

"Aw, see what you did now?" Hal said from behind Vera. "Now it's your fault she's all watery like this."

Vera waggled her finger at Hal. "You just leave us alone here, Haldon. I'll sort this out and tell you what you did wrong."

"I ain't done nothing wrong," Hal said.

"We'll see."

Hal patted Vera on the shoulders and leaned in and kissed her on the cheek. Vera shooed him away with her hand. He shook his head. "It's my tavern!"

"And who runs the kitchen?" she demanded, fixing him with a harsh stare. "It's as much mine as yours, and don't you forget that."

"How can I when you don't let me forget anything?"

Hal's boots thumped over the floorboards and then Carth heard the sound of the bell tinkling over the door before it swung shut.

Vera let out a soft huff. "Damn that man and his strays."

Carth managed to swallow, forcing back the lump in her throat. "Strays?"

Vera patted the table and shook her head. "You think you're the first one he's brought in? All that fighting outside the city brings them in, but I think the man has a way of attracting them, I do. Better here than the alternative, the gods know that's for sure," Vera sighed. "Come on. If you're going to be with us, then it's best that you get settled in. I can see you been through something today. We'll let you rest and then you'll have to start earning your keep."

"How? Why?" she asked.

31

The old woman groaned as she stood, the bench scraping across the wood floor with a scream, and waited for Carth to follow. "We'll talk about that later. For now, you come along."

Carth glanced at the cup of tea and took a small sip before standing and following Vera. With her father missing and her mother dead, what choice did she have?

———

Carth awoke to a thumping in the small room Vera had left her in. There were no windows in the room, a fact that had left Carth's heart beating wildly when she saw Vera intended to leave her here, but the top bunk she'd pointed for her to take appeared clean, and the mattress was soft enough, if not her own. She'd managed to sleep, though she didn't know how long.

The door to the room slammed open and two children raced in. Carth rolled back in the bed, trying to hide herself from them as long as possible. One of the children—a boy who looked no older than nine or ten, with a hooked nose and lanky hair—dropped onto the bed beneath her own. Another, a younger boy with curly brown hair, took the bed opposite, sitting almost carefully.

"Sleep? How she think we gonna sleep?" the boy beneath her said.

"She said you *should* sleep," the other corrected.

"Why you always gotta be so proper, Kel? You live down by the docks the same as me."

32

Kel crawled back into the bed so that Carth couldn't see him as clearly. "Not for long. I'm going to find them."

"You're here for the same reason as me, and until Hal finds your family, you'll be here. Don' forget that we're strays. You're 'bout as likely to find your pa as I'm to find Assage."

"Careful," Kel said. "You shouldn't mention the gods so easily."

The other boy grunted. One of his feet started kicking the wall in a steady rhythmic way. *Thump. Thump-thump. Thump.* "Not my god, now, is he? This damn *place* isn't mine, is it?"

Carth crawled forward, close enough that she could peer over the edge of the bed. Kel rested with his knees bent to his chest, staring blankly forward. He had on tattered pants and his boots looked to be too large for his feet, but it was the introspective way he sat that caught Carth's attention.

"Assage is the one true god," Kel said.

The other boy kicked the wall harder and laughed. "One god? Maybe since we came here, but my family taught me to worship the three. That's why my hands are nimble. It keeps the gods happy."

"What we do won't make any god happy."

The other boy kicked the wall again. "Havin' a full belly makes me happy, and if that's what they ask..."

"What happens when you're caught, Etan? What then?"

"You don't get caught. That's what."

Kel sat silently, not prodded further into the conversation.

Carth moved toward the back wall, trying to stay out of sight. Were these the other strays Vera had mentioned? If they were, what did Vera and Hal ask of them? They seemed well enough, and unharmed, that whatever they wanted couldn't be all bad, could it?

"Now you're going silent on me?" Etan asked. He kicked the wall again, and it sounded like it moved up the wall, toward the upper bunk. There came a kick beneath her, one that struck the bottom of the bunk and sent her into the air. Carth bit back her reaction, but must have said something. Etan scrambled from the lower bunk and stood on the edge, peering at Carth. "What have we got here?" His breath smelled of dried meat, a foul odor that drifted to her. Etan looked over his shoulder toward Kel. "We got another one here, Kel. Climb up here and take a look."

Carth gripped the knife in her fist. She'd been afraid to release it when she'd been with Vera, and Hal must have known but hadn't seemed to care about the fact that she had one of the A'ras's knives. She held it ready, not sure what Etan would try.

"Leave him be, Etan. You know what the last one ended up being like."

Etan smirked. "Not a him this time. Get up here and look!"

Carth heard the sound of Kel climbing from his lower bunk and then he stood next to Etan, his hair rising into view first. He had deep brown eyes that were the color of the dirt tilled on farms outside the city. When he breathed out, his breath smelled of mint or spices, odors that reminded her of the tea Vera had served.

"What you think, Kel? That's a girl, isn't it?"

Carth tucked the knife into her sleeve and swung her legs around, making a point of kicking toward Etan as she did. He had to jump away so that she didn't catch him with her sandaled feet. "I *am* a girl," she said.

Kel covered his mouth as he laughed and jumped down. Etan collected himself pretty quickly and punched Kel in the shoulder. "See? What did I tell you! Where do you think she came from? She's not Reshian like us—"

Kel cut him off with a shake of his head. "Maybe we ask her?"

Etan turned his attention to Carth and his eyes narrowed. "Where did you come from, girl?"

First Vera and Hal, and now these two kept addressing her as *girl*? "I have a name."

"What is it?" Kel asked.

Etan leaned forward as he waited for her to answer.

She glanced from one to the other. What did it matter if she shared her name with them? She wouldn't be here long. Now that she'd rested—and managed to stop crying—she knew that she couldn't stay here. She still didn't—and couldn't—believe that her father was missing. He might not have shown at their meeting place, but that didn't mean something had happened to him. If he wasn't there, she might be able to find him at their home.

"See? Can't even answer right."

"My name is Carth," she said.

"Carth?" Etan repeated the name, adding a harsher sound to the beginning of her name than was supposed to be there. Her mother always told her that she had a beautiful name, one that came from their homeland, a place they had left long ago. Carth might not have ever met anyone else with a name like hers, but she believed her mother.

Yet her full name was too much, too long for her. Carth suited her in ways that Carthenne did not.

She jumped down from the top bunk. From above, Etan had looked smaller than her, but now that she was down here, she realized that he stood at least a hand higher. Kel was closer in height to her, taller if she counted how high his hair stood.

Etan smirked at her again. "How'd you end up here, Carth?" he asked.

"An accident," she said.

She started forward, but Etan didn't move.

Kel glared at him, but the taller boy ignored it. "What kind of accident leaves a girl down here by the docks?"

"What kind of thing leaves a boy like you down here by the docks?" she asked back. But she knew the answer to that. Even though she'd only been in Nyaesh six months, she knew that boys near the docks were either beggars, often orphans from the war, or they worked as thieves. She'd overheard her father speaking of the Thevers, a band of smugglers the A'ras never managed to corral—too busy with their fight outside the city, Carth supposed—and she knew they came in and out of the river port and that many of their members came from the boys along the docks. Was that what Etan and Kel were?

"Probably the same as you," Etan shot back. "What are you hiding from?"

"I'm not hiding from anything," she said.

Etan laughed. "No? Then what are you doing here, if you're not hiding from nothing? Maybe you think you're too good to be down here. Next you're gonna tell me that you don't belong."

"I don't belong."

Etan laughed again. "Keep tellin' yourself that. Lyin' don't make the truth any easier to bear, at least that's what my ma used to tell me. What kind of lies did your ma tell you?"

Carth swallowed the lump that came to her throat, and Etan laughed as she pushed past him and rushed to the door.

Outside, she found a long hall. Carth hurried along the hall and threw open the door at the end. She hurried through another couple of doors before reaching one that finally led outside. A nearly full moon shone overhead, and a chill wind gusted in from the river, making her wish that she had a coat, but she hadn't needed one in the warmth of the morning when she'd left her home.

She heard the sound of boots along the cobbles behind her and ducked into an alley, glancing back to see Kel chasing her. He looked up the street, missing her hiding place in the shadows, and started up. Carth hesitated long enough for him to disappear, and then ran the opposite direction, racing away from the docks and toward her home, praying that her father would be there.

———————————

Carth sat in a crumpled heap outside the only home she had ever known. As she had run back toward the house, she'd allowed herself the growing excitement and belief that her father would be there, waiting with a fire glowing in the hearth, a stew bubbling softly in the flames, preparing herself for his anger and frustration, but ultimately his relief that she'd returned.

The home had been empty.

Not only empty, but someone else had been there before her, tearing through her family's belongings, leaving clothing ripped and the books her mother had painstakingly collected over the years and carted with them as they moved from city to city torn and thrown to the ground. Other belongings were strewn across the floor and then trampled underfoot. Her father had not been here—if he had, he would not have left it like this.

She had paused in the back room, sitting on her parents' bed, letting even more tears come. They streaked down her face even now, wet reminders of what she'd lost. But they were the last. She would cry no more.

Whoever had been here had searched for something. Carth didn't know what might be valuable to anyone else. The only things in the home of worth were the books, and they would only be valuable to certain people. Carth searched through the pile on the floor, realizing that three were missing—three that her mother had prized above all else because they had come with her when she'd left Ih-lash. She searched through the piles, wondering if whoever had been here might have taken them, before remembering the other storage place her mother had used.

Inside her room, she found things less destroyed than the rest of the home. Her sheets were thrown back and her few belongings were tossed onto the floor, including a small wooden carving her father had made for her long ago, but the room was otherwise undisturbed. Carth knelt on the floor, running her hand along the wall between her parents' room and hers, until she felt the slight dimple in the wood and pressed. A small panel opened.

Carth had discovered this hiding spot entirely by accident when she'd fallen in her room once, slamming her backside against the wall. She had considered keeping some of her valuables inside it, but decided against it when she saw that her mother used it as a place to store her favorite books. Over time, Carth had paid attention to what books her mother placed inside the panel, thinking that they might change, but they never did. It was always the same three books.

They were still there.

Carth pulled them out and clutched them to her chest, thinking about her mother. The books were written in Ih, a language Carth had not yet learned. Her mother always promised to teach her later, and now there would not be a later.

She tucked them into the pockets of her dress. Pausing to grab the carved piece from the floor, she made her way back out of the home. She couldn't stay here, not without her father and mother, and not with it destroyed as it was.

The front entrance no longer even looked like her home,

not with the pages strewn all around and with the stink of char burning in the hearth, a scent she hadn't noticed when she'd first come in.

Carth lingered long enough to turn to the fire. The logs within had long since burned out, leaving nothing more than a stain of ash. She traced her finger through the ash, thinking of how her father would have stirred the embers, drawing forth a larger flame. Now it would remain darkened until someone else came in here and cleared out the remains of her home.

She couldn't stay here. Not anymore.

But where would she go? What could she do now?

The only thing she could think to do was to return to Vera and Hal's place, and that meant making her way back down to the docks and suffering through whatever Kel and Etan might put her through.

The alternative was staying on the street.

More than any other lesson her parents had taught, Carth had learned about the streets of cities like Nyaesh, and how unsafe they could be. That was the entire point of the games, the reason that they had warned her to be careful.

Without their help, she needed to be extra careful, only she wasn't entirely sure how. When she'd trailed her mother or tried to find her father when he hid, there had always been an end planned. Now there was no end, and this was nothing like their games. If there were rules, she would have to discover them on her own.

She left the house reluctantly and wandered back toward the river and the docks in something of a haze. When she reached the tavern and crawled back onto the bunk, she ignored the two boys back in the room, trying to hide the tears flowing from her eyes and trying not to think about what she would do now that her parents were gone.

Chapter 4

"You don't have to do it," Kel explained to Carth as they stood along the edge of the road near the docks.

The morning was busy and the street carried more traffic than she was accustomed to seeing, but then this was a different part of the city, one where she had rarely spent any time. Though they'd chosen the market as a meeting place, mostly because it was public, her mother had made it clear that the docks were dangerous and the taverns along the docks equally dangerous. What should Carth make of the fact that Vera and Hal ran one of those taverns?

"I still don't understand what you're telling me to do," Carth said.

Etan leaned against one of the nearby buildings, his lids half-closed, making it appear as if he were sleeping standing up rather than surveying the street. "Probably should just return to where you came from," he suggested.

Carth turned away, hiding her eyes so that they wouldn't see the tears welling in them. She wouldn't allow either of them to see how they affected her. Her parents had taught her to be stronger than that.

"Look at all these people on the street," Kel said, seemingly ignoring Etan's comment. "Most have plenty, not like us. All you're going to do is take a little. Scraps. That's all."

"Stealing."

Etan swung his gaze to her. "Not stealing. Didn't you hear him? Taking scraps. We're strays. That's what we do."

"I don't understand how."

"Watch," Etan said.

He lumbered into the street, making as if to cross. As he did, he collided with another man, one with a plain wool cloak that reminded Carth of her father. Etan made a show of apologizing and then went on his way, hurrying off along the street.

"What was that about?" Carth asked.

"Just wait," Kel told her.

They stood waiting until Etan came through an alley and surprised her. He pulled a small leather pouch from his pocket and shook it. The unmistakable sound of coins jingled inside. "Not all have a purse, but if they do, then you just take it."

"Scraps," Kel explained.

"How did you do it?" Carth asked.

Kel bumped into her. As he did, his hand darted into her pocket.

Carth grabbed it and twisted it back, bending his wrist.

"Let me go!" he snapped.

"What do you think you were doing?"

"I was *trying* to show you how to do what we call the bump and lift, but as you seem to know it already, maybe I don't need to!"

She released his hand and he rubbed his wrist. She shouldn't have been so rough with him, but she had the A'ras knife in her pocket, as well as one of her mother's books. She didn't want to risk Kel accidentally stabbing himself, and she didn't want to lose the book either.

"Sorry. I didn't know what you were doing."

Etan shook his head, an amused smiled coming to his face. "She's not going to get enough scraps to keep Vera happy."

"Vera wants me to do this?" she asked suspiciously. When she'd offered her a place to stay, Vera had mentioned that Carth would have to work for her keep, and she had sent her out with breads and small crafts to sell. This didn't seem like anything the gentle older lady would want her to do.

Kel only shrugged. "She gives us a place to stay and food to eat. There's a price to it."

Carth looked at the loaves of bread on the side of the street where Kel and Etan had left them. "We can sell the bread…"

Etan grunted. "No one buys *that*. You think we'd ever get enough to keep her happy if we didn't find scraps like this?"

Etan glanced at Kel and shrugged. "You can try, but when you can't sell enough to make her happy, then what will you do? Where will you go, Carth?" he taunted.

44

What alternative did she have? She couldn't live alone yet. Not at her age, and not as a girl, so having a place like Vera gave her was the only option, wasn't it? And did it matter if she took a few coins here and there?

Carth tried not to think of what her parents would have said to her about it, but then, her parents had taught her about following closely and avoiding detection, games that she would now have to put to use for a different reason. Her parents might have been disappointed, but they would have wanted her safe, and they would have wanted her fed. If she was required to do this in order to have safety and food, then she would do it.

"How do you pick your target?" she asked.

Kel shrugged. "Not much to it. Find someone who looks like they have enough coins, and then you go after them."

She met his eyes. "And no one catches you?"

"That's the point of the bump. You do it well and they think it's all an accident. You do it wrong and you could get caught with your hand in someone's pocket. Be crafty and quick and no one will ever know." A smile spread on his face. "Besides, no one wants to admit they might have let some kids steal from them."

"Aren't there safer ways?" she asked.

"If you find another way, you're welcome to it," Etan said.

Carth waited, expecting him to say something more, but he didn't.

"Just see what you can do," Kel suggested. "And be ready to run." Etan grinned at the comment.

Carth stepped away from the shadows of the building and surveyed the street. They expected her to fail, and she might. This wasn't anything that she had ever attempted before, and she wasn't entirely sure that she would be able to do it. But she needed to try, and if she could, then she would have a place to stay. That was worth more than anything.

She identified a man with a well-cut jacket, trying not to think about the fact that it was the kind of jacket her father would have worn. He moved toward Doland Street, away from the docks.

Carth crept behind him and glanced back to see Kel and Etan watching her intently before she disappeared behind a building. She could bump this man, but that would only risk him grabbing her. There had to be a way for her to slip past him without him grabbing onto her, maybe without him even noticing that she was there.

There was one game where her father wanted her to slip a flower into her mother's hair while she sat reading. Carth had never gotten all that good at it. Sliding a flower into her hair required a careful touch, and a subtle connection. And it was different than what Carth would attempt now.

But it was the only thing that she had to compare.

Carth approached the man carefully and dipped her hand toward his pocket. She had to move quickly or others on the street would notice her, but not so quickly that the man would feel her presence in his pocket.

She slipped in, feeling the edges of the wool of his jacket. The pocket was empty.

The man paused.

Carth slipped off to the side, her heart hammering in her chest.

Was this really what she would do? Did she really want to become a thief?

Not a thief, she decided. She was a stray collecting scraps. Putting it that way made it easier for her to go back after the man when he continued his way up the street.

This time, she reached quickly into his other pocket and felt a smooth leather purse. Carth grabbed it and pulled it free, spinning to the side and ducking against the wall of the nearest shop as she did.

She gripped the purse tightly, her heart still pounding.

The man continued up the street before pausing again, this time as if he had noticed something.

Carth hid on the side of the street and watched. Enough other people separated her from him that he would be unlikely to notice her, but she could keep him in sight. He patted his pocket before reaching his hand inside. When he realized that his purse was missing, his face darkened and he turned, heading back down Doland Street as he made his way toward the docks.

Carth slipped off onto a side street. She passed a few shops: a butcher with the scent of smoked meat coming from within, a baker nearby that had the scent of fresh bread that made her stomach rumble, and even an herbalist, the type of shop her mother would have been most interested in.

She wandered past the shops, glancing in windows, but doing so only reminded her that she wandered without her parents. Her mother had loved visiting the different shops in

Nyaesh, even if she wasn't able to purchase much. Her father had found them more a necessity than anything but had gone with her, never wanting to let her be alone in the city. He hadn't wanted Carth to be alone in the city either.

Would the pain of losing them ever fade?

She reached the end of the street and found a narrow road that would lead back to the docks. Fewer shops lined this one. Mostly there were homes, though a few stores were here. Carth flipped open the purse and counted the coins within, noting that there were a few copper nils and a pair of silver vens. Even a single gold san glinted at the bottom of the purse. She ran her thumb over it, feeling the ridges stamped on it, an image of the palace on one side and the seal of the royal family of Nyaesh on the other.

She'd never seen a gold coin before. And now she had one, stolen from another.

This wasn't scraps. This was stealing.

But hadn't the A'ras stolen from her and forced her to do this? Hadn't they taken her family from her?

Thinking of it that way made it much easier for her to go on.

———

By evening, Carth had collected from three others, each time finding that it was easier. Her parents had in some ways prepared her for running through the street and collecting scraps. She didn't think that her parents had been thieves, but why, then, had they essentially taught her to do this so well?

She reached the tavern as the sun dipped into the horizon, glittering off the river with streamers of orange and red that were more beautiful than this part of the city had a right to be, especially as she walked toward the Wounded Lyre with her pockets full of coins taken from others.

Guilt worked through her the closer she came to the tavern. What if this wasn't what Vera had wanted her to do? She had taken Kel and Etan at their word that Vera required her to collect a certain amount, but what if they had only said that to play a prank on her? She wouldn't put it past Etan. Kel seemed to have a gentler soul, but what did she really know about him? Not enough to know whether he would be complicit in some plan to trick her into something.

Carth sighed and shifted the coin purses to a different pocket, leaving the lightest one separate. That one had a few coppers only, few enough that she actually didn't feel guilty taking it, especially considering the man she had taken it from had a long silver chain with a symbol marking him as one of the Vellan, servants to the royal family. They were well paid, and arrogant. Carth hadn't minded sneaking from him.

"Where have you been?"

She spun, surprised that Etan would have managed to sneak up on her so easily. Kel stood a step behind him, watching her with a curious expression. Had they expected her to get caught?

"Doing what you told me I needed to be doing," she said.

"You've been gone the whole day!" Etan said.

Carth shrugged.

"Vera has asked about you. We told her you ran off again."

"I didn't run off."

"How were we supposed to know? You didn't come back."

She held up the small purse and shook it. The few coppers inside jingled, reminding her of the sound above Vera's door. "I brought this back."

Etan looked over to Kel. "See? She could do it fine. You were worried that she'd get snatched."

"I wasn't worried," Kel said. "I figured she'd return before nightfall is all. Especially with all the A'ras activity."

Etan shot him a look. "Don't talk about them."

"You can say their name, Etan."

"You'll draw their attention by talking about them. Doing that is dangerous."

Kel didn't argue, instead falling silent.

"This take you all day to get?" Etan asked Carth. He reached for the pouch, but she pulled it back. It was hers now. She might not have earned it in the traditional sense, but she *had* earned it.

"It took me long enough," Carth said. She resisted the urge to touch her other pocket, where she held the two other coin purses, one with enough money to keep her fed for nearly a month. If she could keep this up, she might be able to find a way to get back on her own, even if she was a young girl.

"Did you get caught?" Etan asked.

"I'm here, aren't I?" Carth said.

He grunted. "Just because you're here doesn't mean that you didn't almost get caught. First time Kel tried the bump, he was grabbed. Barely managed to get away. I think it took him nearly a dozen tries before he managed to lift the first purse. Now he's still got slow hands, but he's better at it than he was."

"I'm better than Gustan."

Etan shot him a hard look. "Don't talk about Gustan."

"What happened to him?"

Etan shoved her, knocking her to the ground. "We don't talk about Gustan, do you hear me?"

Carth could only nod in shock.

Etan stared down at her for a long moment before starting away. "Better find Vera. She'll want to know how many scraps you were able to find. Be thankful you lifted any."

Kel watched her for a brief moment before he chased after Etan, leaving Carth lying on the ground near the river, confused about what she had missed.

Chapter 5

The inside of the tavern hummed with activity. Carth crept along the wall, keeping in the shadows. She had long ago mastered the art of hiding in plain sight, disappearing into shadows, practically *willing* herself to remain unseen. Those skills had made Kel smile but had made Etan envious.

The din of voices helped her remain hidden, and the fact that she was young helped keep eyes off her. Carth had discovered the way to move silently when trailing her mother, but she had mastered it in the last month. She barely made a sound as she moved from table to table, and her touch had grown deft. She now separated patrons of this tavern from their wallets as easily as she had once slipped between crowds, trying to reach her mother.

As she approached the nearest table, the man started to turn while she reached for his wallet.

Carth feigned falling forward, rolling to the side and faking tears. They no longer fell as easily as they once had, but then she hadn't cried—really cried—since leaving her home for the last time and making her way back to Vera and

Hal's. The older woman had welcomed her in without a word and made a point of shooing Etan away, giving her space. So far, they hadn't even questioned where she had gone or why she had returned.

Scrambling to her feet, she scuttled across the floor until she could hide along the wall. Carth took a moment to survey the room again. Vera would be displeased if she was caught, but then Vera believed that Carth sold her breads and crafts for the coins she brought back each day. The few occasions she *hadn't* returned with enough coin, she'd seen the disappointed look on Vera's face, one that told her how upset she was. The woman never used violence to demonstrate her displeasure, only a stern expression and sharp words. Carth had come to dislike those nearly as much as the gentle rebukes she once would have gotten from her mother.

Across the tavern, Etan worked much the same way as Carth, though he didn't have the same deft touch and had to bump into patrons as he worked his way through. Carth didn't need anything quite like his bruising method, preferring to sneak in and then back out before anyone was the wiser.

Theft was common along the docks, which made their work along the street easy enough, but it was equally common in the taverns along the docks. When she'd visited a few of the other taverns, she had discovered that there were others like her, others taking scraps. It had surprised her at first, but the more she watched for it, the more she recognized those along the docks most responsible for taking coin. A sort of truce existed, one where you worked only your tavern, which was another justification for Etan and Kel. If they didn't take coins, someone else would.

She ducked away from the wall and slipped her hand into a pocket of an older man before withdrawing with the coin purse within. From the weight of it, Carth knew that she'd probably taken her allotment for the night. She knew to be careful not to steal *too* much. Too much risked drawing Vera's attention, as well as the reputation of the tavern.

Carth made her way toward the kitchen. Now that she had full pockets, it was time for a full stomach. At one table sat a plain-faced young man with a finely woven cloak practically draped across the table, his eyes focused on the dark-haired woman sitting across from him. A gold bracelet that hung from his wrist matched the flash of gold around his neck. That much gold would make it likely that his pockets were equally heavy. Grabbing his purse might give her a night free, and *that* was really what she wanted.

Weaving around the table, she made a point of moving erratically, intending to slide back around to the man. When she turned, he still perched on his chair, his gaze fixed on the woman.

How could she not attempt to grab his purse?

Carth slipped forward and reached for his pocket.

As she did, he spun, almost as if expecting her movement, and grabbed at her wrist. Carth had a moment to catch the deep curiosity in his eyes and had a flash of recognition before she jerked her arm free and darted toward the kitchen.

She didn't bother to see if he would chase.

Inside the kitchen, the heat from the oven was nearly oppressive. She hurried to the back door and crawled onto a nearby stool to peek through the small cutout in the door through which she could just make out the inside of the tavern. She couldn't see the man at the table from this angle, but for a moment, she thought it had been Jhon, the man who had tried to grab her when she saw her mother in the street, then chased her to the temple.

Why would he be here?

"Get down from there!"

At the hard edge of Vera's words, Carth scrambled down. "Sorry, Vera."

She waved a spoon at her. "What do you think you're doing, anyway? Aren't you supposed to be out wiping tables and collecting scraps?"

Carth smiled. That was what Vera called it when she had her strays roaming the tavern. They collected scraps of food as they cleaned the tables, wiping them off so that others could use them. That was the reason Etan thought it particularly amusing to refer to their *other* activity by the same name.

"Kel is taking care of it tonight. And I…"

Vera's eyes narrowed in that warm way she had. Carth hated that she had to lie to her.

"What happened?"

"I… I thought I saw someone I recognized. From before." She'd never explained to Vera or Hal what had happened, and neither had asked for answers. A few other children had come through for a day, sometimes two, but they never stayed longer. Carth had discovered almost all of them came from outside the city and moved to a place of safety, but she still didn't know why.

"Go on to bed if you want," Vera said. "Tomorrow looks to be a busy night, what with the festival and all. You probably never collected scraps during a Evenstorm Festival, but most of the men are half-drunk by the time they show up. Should be a busy night."

"Yes, Vera."

As Carth started from the kitchen, Vera caught her hand. "You know I'm always willing to listen."

Carth swallowed, tears welling up for the first time in weeks. She ran from the kitchen, risking another glance back toward the door into the tavern, thankful that it created space between her and whoever was out there.

Once in the street, Carth slipped into the shadows created by the streetlamps, preferring to fade into the darkness rather than walk openly. While here, she could remain hidden, avoiding any of the crowds moving away from the docks. Night drew like a shroud overhead, dark sheets of clouds drifting above her blocking the moonlight. Wind gusted from the north, unusual for Nyaesh.

Carth gripped the hilt of the knife stolen from the A'ras. In the weeks she'd lived with Vera and Hal, the knife and the books reclaimed from her childhood home had become her prized possessions. The knife because it symbolized the vengeance that she intended to claim for her parents as well as a means to achieve it, and the books because they were her only connection to her mother, other than the ring she now wore on a loop of twine around her neck.

She stopped at the same place she stopped each night, lingering outside the home that had once been hers. Lights glowed within, and the sound of voices drifted from the open windows. The home had remained empty for nearly two weeks, but when it became apparent that no one would return, Carth hadn't been surprised that someone else moved in. She had never stopped by in the daylight, and didn't really want to. She didn't want to risk the possibility that she might see the people who had taken over her home.

But each night she managed to get free, she came here, if only for a few moments. It served as a reminder. With each day, she felt a growing desire for answers that might never come, but she had something that would help her find what she wanted. She had a name.

Felyn had been there the day her mother had died. He had been responsible for the deaths of the A'ras. And he was likely responsible for what had happened to her mother, possibly even her father.

All she wanted was to know what had happened, but how could she, a girl of no more than twelve, find the answers she needed? Not by sneaking around Vera's tavern, taking scraps from her patrons.

The temple was the only other place she visited as often. It was always empty, even more so than it had been that night, reminding her of how her home had been empty. It was times like this, when she stared at her old home, the longing for her missing family filling her chest and gnawing at her stomach, that she wondered what would become of her. When her parents were alive, she had never taken the time to think about it, but now that they were gone, what would she do? She couldn't steal from the patrons in the tavern indefinitely. Eventually she would grow up, and she didn't know what Vera or Hal intended for her then.

Rather than making her way toward the temple, tonight she wandered toward the small square where her mother had died. Carth rarely went back there. The memories were too painful. When she had returned to the square, she found herself drawn to the small wall and would sit next to it and simply stare as people wandered by.

Two streetlamps glowed with soft orange light on either end of the wall. Carth crouched outside the wall, leaning against it with her hand tucked in her pocket as she gripped the knife while watching people making their way through the street. This section of the city didn't have the same number of taverns found near the docks. Mostly there were shops here, and the people passing by looked as if they lived and worked nearby.

A flash of maroon caught her attention and she tensed. She sat far too openly and didn't like the idea that one of the A'ras might see her, especially as she held one of their knives. They had no reason to harass her, but that didn't always mean they wouldn't.

The man made his way quickly through the plaza.

Carth watched him as he did. It was rare to find the A'ras walking alone. The bastards always moved in pairs, making getting revenge difficult, but alone...

She stood and moved after him, careful to mask the

sounds of her steps. At night, even with her best effort, her feet still seemed to thud across the pavers. Carth found the shadows but wasn't able to hide nearly as well as she wanted.

The A'ras moved quickly and made no effort to hide his passing. Others in the street shrunk back or turned away, but not Carth. Were she playing a game as she had with her parents, he would have lost. It was far too easy to track him, nothing like trying to keep up with her mother. Her father was even harder.

As she neared, she pulled the knife from her pocket.

Her heart fluttered and she forced it to slow. Having nerves now wouldn't serve her, not when she finally had a chance to do something about what had happened to her family. This would be the beginning.

Unless she failed. If the A'ras noticed her following, she knew that he would have no difficulty dispatching her. Even without their magic, they were skilled swordsmen and she was nothing more than a little girl. But if she came at him quietly and snuck up behind him, she might be able to sink the knife into his back before he even knew she was there.

Barely ten paces away, the man turned a corner. Behind him, Carth paused, her face pressed against the cool stone as she peered around the building, a wave of nausea rolling through her.

The A'ras lay on the ground, unmoving.

Carth scanned for who else might be there but saw nothing.

She waited, half-expecting the man to stand, but when he didn't, she realized that someone else had gotten to him first.

Her fluttering heart began to race. The only person she had ever heard of attacking the A'ras had been Felyn. The rest of the city feared them, and for good reason.

Could that man be here?

If he was, Carth wanted to be somewhere else. As much as she wanted to know why her mother had been killed and what had happened to her father, she had no misconceptions that she could handle herself when it came to Felyn, especially when he had dispatched three A'ras as quickly and easily as he had.

Nothing else moved.

Not Felyn, then. Or if it was him, he had already departed.

Carth crept forward, keeping her body crouched and her muscles tensed so that she could bolt away at the first sign of anyone else, but there was nothing.

Blood pooled from the A'ras's neck. She tipped his head back and noted the long slit across his throat. Seeing a man dead like this should bother her, but this was one of the A'ras. She had a hard time feeling anything for him. Searching his body, hoping for another knife or something, she discovered that even his curved sword was missing.

How had someone been here and cleared him of weapons so quickly? She had only been a few steps behind, not far enough back that she wouldn't have been able to see it when someone attacked and then searched the body.

There was a sash of red wrapped around his upper arm, a marker of the A'ras.

Carth untied it and ran her fingers along the silky surface

a moment before tucking it into her pocket. Now the only thing that marked him as one of them was the small tattoo of three stars across his right hand.

Sounds came from behind her and Carth scurried forward. She didn't want to be caught in the open with one of the A'ras dead. Once she reached a nearby alley, she paused and watched. A young couple happened upon the A'ras first, their shocked gasp drawing more attention until others came. Someone must have noticed the tattoos on his hand and understood what they meant because everyone began backing away, eventually leaving the body untouched on the stones.

Carth waited, wondering if any of the A'ras would claim him, but when the distant temple bell tolled twice, she decided she needed to return to Vera's tavern. As she made her way back, she thought she heard footsteps trailing behind her, but when she turned to look, she saw nothing.

With each step, the sense that someone trailed after her increased until she started sprinting, only slowing when the crowd around her thickened and the stink of fish from the docks told her that she neared the tavern.

Chapter 6

The elderly man sat with his back to her, a stack of coins on the table making him a clear mark, but it was the two men on either side of him that made her pause. A thick-armed man whose floral tattoos marked him as being from Garvain kept his eyes roving around the tavern, never settling in one place. The other man, a thin, compact man wearing a plain brown cloak, stared straight ahead. Strangely, she found herself drawn to him most of all.

"Aren't you going to make a play at it?" Kel asked.

Carth rubbed her eyes. She was tired from lack of sleep. Etan had kicked the bottom of her bunk repeatedly throughout the night, thinking it funny to keep her awake. He'd thought it even funnier as she'd stumbled along the streets throughout the day, too tired to keep her focus as she tried grabbing at purses, but struggled too much. She kept going back to the place where she'd left the sash, burying it under rocks near the shore.

"I don't think he's the best target." She hated letting scraps like that get away, but what would she risk if she attempted to get past his two companions, and tired at that? The bigger man was more likely to catch her, but she had experience moving quickly with men like him. That was one advantage to her size. The other man made her more uncomfortable.

"Etan said—"

Carth spun to Kel and jabbed a finger into his chest. He took a step back, grabbing at his shirt where she poked. "I don't care what Etan said," she whispered. Even irritated, she still had to be careful that she didn't speak too loudly here, preferring instead to let the voices in the Wounded Lyre keep her voice obscured. "If you think he's such an easy target, then *you* grab at his pocket."

Carth slipped away from him, staying near the walls, where she could observe the entire tavern. After the previous night, she almost didn't want to collect enough scraps so that she could leave the tavern. When she'd reached her bed, it had taken her hours for her heart to slow, and she'd still been awake when Kel and Etan came into the room. Etan made no attempt to keep his voice down in spite of Kel shushing him. There was something more going on in the city with the A'ras than she knew, and she wanted to find out who else might be targeting them.

As she moved away from the table, she had a crawling sensation between her shoulder blades, one she recognized from the games played with her parents, one that made her think that someone watched her.

Slowly lowering herself, she discovered the smaller man looking in her direction. Carth shivered. Had she attempted to grab the old man's coins, she had little doubt that he would have seen her.

She continued to move away from the table. There were other tables where she could work, though she'd already made a pass through here, so finding additional scraps without attracting attention would be difficult. Better to return to the kitchen, take a few bites, and come back when there had been some turnover. That would be safest, but Vera would frown on it.

A low-pitched voice caught her attention. Not so much the tone or a sense of familiarity, but the content. "You hear another of them bastards got cut last night?"

Carth looked for who spoke and found a younger man with a wild shock of dark hair on his head, leaning forward intently. The three others at his table all sipped tall mugs of ale, two of them with eyes already glazed over. They might be drunk enough for her to pilfer from them, but they had the look of sailors, men without much money. More than that, Vera had warned her to stay clear of men like that.

"Careful, Bren," the man across from him said.

Bren raised his glass and took a long drink. "Why should I be careful here? There's nothing but drunks here."

"You're here," the man next to him said.

"I'm a drunk." Bren took another drink. "Shouldn't we talk about it? After so many getting cut, don't you wonder what's going on?"

"They're still the A'ras," the third man said. His brown eyes looked at the others more clearly, and in the time Carth had been watching, he hadn't touched his drink. "You talk about them and they find out. Best to leave well enough alone, Bren."

The other two men nodded.

Bren finished off his ale and slammed it down. "I'll leave it alone, but you don't need to be so damn scared to even *talk* about it. Especially now, with the Reshian making their presence known." His voice rose as he spoke, and talk at some of the nearest tables began to die down. The sober man grabbed Bren and pulled on his arm, but Bren shook him off. "No reason to be scared down here, Foln. They ain't down here. They're *never* down here." When another man grabbed at him, he stood. "Fine. I'm going."

As Bren weaved his way through the tavern, he bounced off one of the poles and Kel slipped forward, moving too slowly as he slid his hand into Bren's pocket and back out. Bren tripped over Kel and they both fell forward.

"What you think you're doing?" Bren said.

Kel crawled back, his eyes wide.

Bren patted his pocket and Carth watched with growing concern as the man realized that his coin pouch was now in Kel's hand.

"Boy?" Bren thundered.

Carth glanced at the kitchen. If Vera discovered Kel had been caught grabbing scraps, she'd throw him out. She might start to ask about how Carth and Etan managed to bring in so much coin. They all might be out of a place to stay.

Kel continued to scoot away, not saying anything.

The door to the kitchen opened and Vera poked her head out.

The voices in the tavern began to die down as Bren towered over Kel.

Carth darted forward and slipped her hand quickly into Kel's pocket as she helped him up. Bren stormed over to him and shoved Kel away. As he did, Carth quickly dropped the coin pouch and kicked it toward the pole.

"You filchin' from me?" Bren demanded.

Kel shook his head, his gaze going to Carth as he searched for help.

Damn him! Bren didn't have enough coin to begin with, and he was already leaving. Kel knew better than to go after someone like that.

"I felt you grab—"

"Sir?" Carth interrupted.

Bren blinked, slowly turning his gaze away from Kel.

"I think you dropped your purse when you tumbled," she said, motioning toward the pole.

Bren staggered toward the pole and leaned forward, carefully clinging to it for support as he did. He grabbed his purse from the ground and held it up to the light, a confused frown on his face. For a moment, Carth felt a flutter of fear that she'd grabbed the wrong purse, but then Bren shook it and stuffed it back into his pocket.

Conversations in the tavern began to resume. Carth allowed herself a moment to think that he might leave without saying anything else, but Bren took a step toward Kel. Kel didn't move, standing stiff and frozen in place, staring with his wide-eyed expression at the larger man.

"I felt him grabbin'," Bren muttered.

"I think you just bumped into him," Carth suggested as she stepped between man and boy. She looked past him to his now-standing friends, praying that they would take him from the tavern without another incident. "An accident. That's all."

The sober man eyed Carth strangely and then nodded, rushing forward to grab Bren. He pulled on the larger man, dragging him toward the door. "You're drunk, Bren," the man said.

"That's what I told you," Bren answered.

"You said you were *a drunk*. I'm saying you *are* drunk."

Bren grunted as the door opened and he was pulled outside. "Pretty much the same, don' you think?"

The other men with him glanced at Carth and shrugged as they followed the others out of the tavern.

Carth grabbed Kel and pulled him to the kitchen, feeling that crawling sensation between her shoulders again. As she closed the door behind her, she noted the thin man watching her again.

"What was that?" Vera demanded as soon as the door closed. "Did you try to *steal* from one of my patrons?"

Kel hung his head. "I'm sorry, Vera. It was a—"

"An accident," Carth cut in, shooting him a glare to keep him silent. What *had* Kel been thinking? Why would he have risked thieving from a man like Bren? There wasn't likely to be much of value in his purse anyway. Any real coin he had would have been spent on ale throughout the night.

Vera crossed her arms over her chest as she looked from Carth to Kel. "Accident?"

Carth shrugged. "The man was drunk, Vera. He bounced off the pole into Kel when they got tangled up. Can't blame that on Kel."

Vera watched her a long moment before scanning the tavern and then waving her hand. "Get out of here, both of you."

Carth started away from the kitchen. When she reached the door, she realized that Kel hadn't followed.

His hands were clasped together, and he fidgeted with his fingers while looking at her. "Vera," he said.

Vera stood in front of a pot, stirring what smelled like chicken broth, and glanced up. "What is it?"

"It was my fault. I shouldn't have—"

Carth slammed the door to the back of the kitchen open, startling Kel. "You coming?"

The other boy blinked a moment and nodded. "I'm sorry," he mumbled to Vera and ran toward the open door.

When they were through, Carth jabbed him in the chest with her finger. "What was that about?"

"I don't know what you're talking about."

She pulled him down the hall to their room. The floor creaked overhead and footsteps thudded across the boards. Carth lowered her voice and leaned toward Kel. "I saw what you did. What were you thinking, grabbing at that drunk?"

"That's why we're here, isn't it?"

Kel attempted to shoulder past her, but she grabbed his wrist to keep him from getting too far. "That's why we're here, but it's not to get caught. We're only to take scraps. Bren didn't have any scraps for you to claim!" They reached their room and she pushed open the door, stepping aside to let Kel into the room.

"Who's Bren?"

Carth closed the door more firmly than she intended. "Bren was that stupid drunk you decided to steal from. Didn't you even look at him? He barely had enough to pay for his drinks, and then you go and grab for his purse." She planted her fists on her hips as she faced him, waiting for him to answer, but he didn't. A flush rising in his cheeks was all the answer she got. "Well?"

Kel threw himself onto his bed and backed into a corner. "What do you want me to say? I don't recognize scraps as well as you do." He pounded the wall with his fist, turning his back to her. "Stupid thing, anyway. They're not scraps. Just coin from all the drunks they let into their tavern."

Carth took a seat on the edge of his bed. "It's either that or you sell what Vera wants you to sell. It's what we've got to do because we're strays."

"Strays. Etan and I are strays. Not you."

"What's that supposed to mean?"

Kel managed to turn so that he could look at her. His hair stood in disarray, rubbing against the upper bunk. "What do you think it means? You're no stray. Strays are given up. Left. Unwanted." He swallowed and she noted that tears welled in his eyes. "That's not you. I saw the way you were dressed when you came."

"You don't know anything about me!"

"Because you refuse to share!"

The sound of footsteps coming down the hall made her

turn. Was it Etan? She didn't want to have him show up while she argued with Kel. They had been together longer, and she knew which side Etan would take if it came down to it.

"Well?" Kel said.

Carth ignored him and crawled up into the top bunk.

What did he know about her? She wouldn't tell him how she'd seen her mother dead. Or how her father, who was supposed to have been following behind her, playing nothing more than a game, was missing. She refused to tell him that she had been *happy*, really happy, and had lost everything. How did that not make her a stray?

Carth wiped tears from her eyes and pulled the knife from her pocket, setting it next to the pillow. She reached under her pillow and pulled out the books reclaimed from her home, the only scraps she had left of that time.

Forcing herself to control her breathing, she pulled the books to her face. When she inhaled, she could almost smell the remnants of her mother, a connection to that past, a hint of pine and tehla spice that she wished she could find once more.

But she couldn't. There was no more home for her.

Carth didn't even bother opening the books and rested her head on her pillow.

As she tried to sleep, Kel finally spoke again. "Thanks." When she didn't say anything more, she heard him crawl out from his bunk and stand on Etan's, the pressure from his hands pushing down on her bunk. "You didn't have to help me back there, so thanks."

Carth didn't turn to face him. "I thought I was helping another stray," she said. Her hand slipped to the hilt of the knife and she squeezed it, feeling the weight of the handle pressing against her skin.

Kel breathed out heavily. "I'm… I'm sorry. I shouldn't have said that." He stepped down, his boots settling heavily on the floor. "That was quick thinking, what you did."

"I shouldn't have had to."

"You're right," Kel said.

"Don't be stupid again."

Kel was quiet for a moment and she heard him crawling back into his bunk. "I'll try not to."

Carth took a deep breath, pulling her mother's books to her face and inhaling their scent again. When she couldn't sleep, she flipped one open, choosing at random, and left the page open as she settled her head on the book. She might not be able to read Ih, but as she fingered her mother's ring, she could have comfort that her mother had once read these books. For a little while, she didn't feel like the stray that she was.

Chapter 7

Darkness covered the street along the docks as Carth moved as stealthily as she could, each step silent against the night. Kel didn't manage nearly so well, his heavy boots slapping against the cobbles, making nearly as much racket as a horse trotting through the city.

"Do you have to be so loud?" she asked.

Kel jogged up to her, breathing heavily. Even that was loud. "I'm not as quiet as you."

"You're not," she agreed.

"I'm not as quick at grabbing scraps as you either."

Carth veered toward a pool of shadows. They didn't really help keep Kel any quieter, but at least in the shadows they would avoid some detection. "Nope."

"How?" he asked.

Carth paused near a point, the river rushing noisily over rocks. At least here, Kel's voice wouldn't carry quite as well. "How what?"

"You. You weren't a stray before you came to Vera. I know that. So how is it that you manage to walk so much softer than me and have such quick hands? Were you a thief before Vera found you?"

"Vera didn't find me."

"Fine. Hal found you. Pretty much the same."

Carth turned to face the river, listening to the sound of it rushing over rocks as it flowed toward the sea. She could jump in, let the river carry her. She'd learned to swim the surf in places like Darfan and didn't fear the water. If it flowed far enough, she might even make it all the way back to Ih-lash, where she'd been born. She never understood why her parents had left a land they so clearly loved and come to Nyaesh. Whenever she would ask, her mother's response was always the same: *Later*. Now there would be no later.

Kel stood next to her, his shoulder brushing up against hers. "Were you a thief before?" he asked again. She shook her head. "Maybe trained by the A'ras?"

"Careful," she cautioned.

Kel faced her, a smile splitting his mouth. "Funny that you would tell me to be careful. I've seen how you sneak out, come back with full pockets. You never stray this far in the city. Where do you go when you run off?"

"Nowhere. And I wasn't a thief."

Kel studied her face a moment, the moonlight reflecting off his deep brown eyes, making them almost appear black. "If you say so. Doesn't change the fact that you have faster hands than me."

"I didn't see you complaining when I split my collection with you tonight."

Kel grinned again. "I didn't say I'd complain. It's nice to actually collect enough for a change."

"What's that supposed to mean? Vera doesn't care if we don't bring in coins."

"Maybe not, but I can't imagine she likes it when we don't bring in what she wants, either. There's a price to staying with them."

"Yeah? Then what's the price?"

"I don't know. But there has to be something. Vera might not tell us outright, but that don't mean we get a free pass. And if I can't sell enough, then I got to collect scraps."

"But I've seen you collect enough before."

"Have you? I've never really managed to move quickly enough. Most of the time I have to use the bump technique."

"That's a stupid way of collecting. You'd be crashing around the streets."

Kel arched a brow at her. "Yeah? Before you came, that was all we needed. Then you show up and demonstrate your quick hands, collecting scraps that would last a week before."

"Vera doesn't need the money anyway," Carth said. When Kel arched a brow at her, she shrugged. "The Lyre is busy enough that she doesn't need the money to feed us."

The tavern was busy. Most nights it was crowded, with the attached inn managing to rent out its rooms more often than not, especially situated near the river as it was. That much business wouldn't require her to need Carth and the others to bring in much money. Did she have them selling in the street to keep them busy? It would keep them away from the tavern during the day, at least give Vera a chance to cook without them bothering her, and she'd never asked them to stick around to help.

"Where have you been going at night?" Kel asked.

Carth shook herself, pulling her thoughts back to the conversation. "I've just been wandering."

"That's not safe, you know. The A'ras patrol more than they used to. There's something going on outside the city that makes them nervous. You get in the way…"

"I'm safe enough."

"Yeah?" Kel grabbed at her arm quickly and pulled on her. "What happens if—"

The suddenness gave her a flashback to when the man had grabbed her outside the square and covered her mouth. Carth jerked on her arm, tearing it free, while pulling the A'ras knife from her pocket.

Kel raised his hands and took a step back. "What do you think you're doing?"

"I'd ask you the same thing!" She jabbed at him with the knife and he took another step back.

His feet slipped and he started to fall.

Carth jumped for him.

There would be no way for her to reach him. Kel had moved too far from her, but fear for him must have made her quicker than she should have been. She reached him, grabbing for his wrist. For a moment, she had him.

"Don't let me fall!" Kel pleaded.

His wrist began to slip. Carth didn't have a strong enough grip, and he slipped from her, falling into the churning water.

The current pulled at him, too fast for him to swim against.

Cursing, Carth stuffed the knife into her pocket—she wasn't about to lose the one thing that might help her get revenge on the A'ras—and jumped into the river after him.

She was a strong swimmer, but this was madness!

Cold water slapped at her, and the frothy churn tried to pull her under. She kicked, keeping her head above the water, and swam with the current, trying to reach Kel. Each stroke carried her far along the shore. If she wasn't careful, she'd float beyond the city… or more likely, get bashed into the rocks.

Kel popped to the surface not far from her. With another stroke, she reached him and slipped an arm around him, keeping him above the surface.

He coughed and took a hoarse breath. "Carth?"

"Can you swim?"

"Not in this. Water is too fast!"

"It's not too fast. Just kick your legs."

Kel looked at her, his eyes wide and the color drained from his face. "You should have just let me go. Now we're both going to drown."

She started kicking, trying to get to the shore. They'd been pulled to the middle of the river, and the shore looked to be over twenty yards away. "We're not going to drown," she snapped. "But you have to help."

Kel finally started to kick. They moved slowly toward the shore, angling against the fast-moving current. The only advantage to it being night was that none of the shipping boats sailed, leaving the river as a churning black sheet.

"I can't keep going!" Kel cried.

"You have to." Carth's arms had begun to tire and her lungs burned, with each breath feeling like she breathed fire, but she knew the moment she gave up, they would drift along down the river. Much longer, and they would get pulled under.

"Carth—"

He started to slip from her grasp, and she squeezed his sides, trying to hold him in place. She couldn't—she *wouldn't*—lose Kel. It was her fault that he'd fallen in, and she wasn't about to be the reason someone she cared about died.

Carth continued to kick, holding as tightly to Kel as she could. Her vision started to go black and she blinked, trying to clear it, not wanting to lose sight of the shore. It was tantalizingly close now. All she needed was a few more kicks.

Kel slipped from her grip and dropped beneath the water.

Carth cried out.

She stopped swimming and took a deep breath before diving beneath the surface.

Water rushed past her as she tried to swim in place. It was too dark to see Kel. Had she lost him?

Something grabbed at her sleeve.

Kel?

Then Carth was pulled from beneath the water, and with strong strokes, someone dragged her to the shore and threw her up to the top of the rocks. The overwhelming cold finally struck her and she shivered uncontrollably.

Someone had saved her.

"Kel!"

She sat up and saw a man with a dark cloak shaking himself free from the water. "The other will join you soon."

Carth followed the direction of the rushing water along the shore and saw another man carrying a small, unmoving bundle over his shoulder. When he neared, he set Kel down next to Carth. She checked to see that he was breathing, then finally allowed herself to relax.

"Thank you," she said.

The first man stood along the shore, staring out at the river as the other approached. "You should not have gone for a swim so late."

"It wasn't a swim. He fell in."

"And you went with him?"

"I went after him."

The man turned and came toward her. Moonlight filtering through the clouds gave deep shadows to his face, but there was something familiar about him. Had she seen him before? He didn't have the look of the sailors who came through the docks, dropping off shipments on their way farther down the river, and he didn't have the stink of the local fishermen, but he'd been a strong enough swimmer to pull her from the water.

"You went after him in the dark and this late in the season?"

Carth didn't know how to respond. It was foolish what she had done, but letting Kel drown because of an accident would have been equally foolish. "I didn't have a choice."

"There's always a choice," the man said.

He took a step toward Carth and she shivered again, this time less certain whether the cold in the air made her shiver. With a sudden pulsing fear in her chest, she searched for signs that he might be one of the A'ras, a sash or a sword, but found nothing. The A'ras wouldn't have gone into the river after someone drowning, anyway. More likely, they would have been the reason someone had been thrown in.

She pulled the knife from her pocket anyway. The blade reflected some of the moonlight, gleaming dully, and the faint edges of a smile pulled on the man's mouth.

"Do you know how to use that?" he asked.

Carth jabbed toward him with it.

He chuckled. "That's one way. Not the only one."

Kel coughed and the man glanced at her knife once more before turning back to his partner, taking a place along the shore, staring at the river as if expecting something to float down it. He wasn't a tall man, nor particularly large, but he stood as if an immovable rock along the shore.

"Carth?" Kel whispered.

"It's me."

"How? What happened?"

"We nearly drowned."

Kel coughed again and started to sit up. He tensed when he saw the two men standing along the shore. Neither moved, and neither spoke.

"I know that. How did we *not*?"

Carth motioned to the men. "They pulled us from the river."

Kel was silent for a while. "We... we should get back."

Carth took a deep breath and felt her heart beginning to slow. Kel was right. They had been gone long enough. If they didn't appear, would Vera or Etan bother coming to look for them?

Kel helped her to stand. Water dripped from her dress and her braid remained saturated and stunk of the river. She'd have to comb it out, and she hoped that her dress dried quickly. Kel looked as miserable as she felt, with his normally thick hair flattened against his face, and his shirt and pants clinging to his body.

He started to grab for her wrist but caught himself. "Come on," he said instead.

Kel started down the street.

Carth glanced at the two men, but they didn't seem to notice. Could she leave without saying anything more to them? They *had* saved their lives. She owed them some sort of thanks, at least.

She approached them slowly, neither man seeming to move, but both tensing as she neared. "Thanks. For saving us, I mean."

The shorter man turned. The shadows cast by the moonlight parted slightly, and Carth realized why he was familiar. She resisted the urge to back away, the desire to run. This was the man from the tavern the night before, the one who had seemed to watch her, staring at her with a gaze that seemed almost knowing as she considered taking scraps from the man with the stack of coins on the table.

His face gave no sign that he recognized her. "Choose a

better time to swim next time," he said.

Carth bobbed her head in a quick nod and turned to run off after Kel. As she did, she had a crawling sensation between her shoulder blades, the same sensation she'd had the night before, when she had been convinced that he watched her. Only, when she risked a glance back, the man once again stared at the river.

She didn't slow her pace until she reached Kel near the edge of the city. Neither spoke much as they slowly made their way back toward the docks of Nyaesh, and to the Wounded Lyre.

Chapter 8

The next few days passed slowly. Kel rarely spoke to Carth, and when he did, it was nothing more than a few terse words, almost as if he was mad at her for what had happened. In some ways, she supposed that it had been her fault. Had she not pulled her knife on him, he might not have stepped too close to the edge of the rock and fallen into the river, but then, had he not grabbed her wrist, she wouldn't have needed to pull her knife on him.

The one time she'd tried to approach him, he'd brushed it off, but the look in his eyes spoke of embarrassment more than anger. How could she help him get past *that*?

Etan noticed the tension between them and, unsurprisingly, favored Kel. The larger boy had never warmed to her, and it seemed that he would not now. When he wasn't tormenting her by kicking her bunk, keeping her from getting even a single good night's sleep, he went out of his way to make collecting scraps more difficult, making a point of interrupting her as she stalked toward different people along the street. More than that, he'd taken to talking to some of the older boys on the street, but whenever she got close, he glared at her until she left him alone.

Carth had given up on the subtle approach and instead went with the bump-and-lift technique. It was a little less graceful than what she preferred, but she didn't have much of a choice with the way Etan interrupted her. She considered using it on him as revenge, taking whatever paltry amount he might have collected, but decided against it. One stray shouldn't steal from another.

The morning of the fourth day after they'd nearly drowned, she found herself tailing the same man as Kel. Their target wore a formal cloak, almost too warm for the weather, and the fine silk hat that covered his head was out of place for the docks. The flash of silver on his wrist had made him an easy mark.

As she approached, her feet padding silently over the cobbles, she heard the steady clopping of Kel's feet.

She shot a look over her shoulder. What did he think he was doing? There was an unspoken agreement that when one of them chose a target, the others stayed away. Kel knew that as well as anyone—he had watched as Etan made certain that she knew.

Kel ignored her as he closed the distance.

Carth turned her attention back to the man she followed. He paused at an intersection, peering in both directions on the side street before hurrying across. Carth waited a moment, giving him space as he went so that he didn't think she followed him, and took the time to grab Kel's wrist.

"What are you doing?" she asked.

He pulled away from her. "Collecting scraps. The same as you."

"Not the same as me. *I* marked him first."

"I don't see it that way."

He started across the street, hurrying after the man without saying anything else.

The comment hurt. What had she done other than help him? Kel was supposed to be her friend—one of the few that she had made while staying with Vera and Hal. She considered choosing a different target; now that she had moved off the River Road, away from the docks, Etan wasn't there to sabotage her collections. But stubbornly, she didn't *want* to find a different mark.

Carth slipped between the crowd as she crossed the street. In spite of the midmorning noise, she could still pinpoint Kel's footsteps, using the tricks she'd learned from her parents. Much like following her mother, when she followed Kel, she was careful to keep her head down and made a point of weaving around the people in the street, avoiding notice as she moved as silently as possible.

She reached the top of a slight rise. In the distance, the domed peak of the temple rose to the east, the top of it gleaming almost gold in the sunlight. To the west, rows of tall houses continued to rise until they reached the palace. She caught sight of the man in his heavy cloak making his way west.

Carth hurried forward, now chasing not only the target, but Kel as well.

When she caught Kel, she bumped into him from behind and sent him sprawling.

He fell to the cobbles, a hurt look on his face. Carth ignored him and slunk after the man. Now it was less about scraps and more about showing Kel that he couldn't treat her that way.

At another intersection, the man paused again before heading across the street, seemingly making his way toward the palace. Carth hurried after him, knowing as she did that she followed too quickly and too closely.

The man turned.

She skidded to a stop, turning aside as if to make it appear that she wanted only to peer into the window of the dress shop she happened to find herself in front of.

Carth studied the reflection off the glass to see the man working his way up the street again. Going after him would be foolish, something that Etan would do. She needed to return to the docks, where she knew the places to hide before sneaking out to collect scraps.

Kel came thundering up behind her, running faster than he should.

"Kel!" She hissed his name as quietly as she could, but he didn't make any effort to slow or look back at her.

The stupid boy would end up getting caught again, and this time there was nothing she could do to protect him, not from a man who looked like he might have half of the royal family in his pocket.

Carth considered simply returning to the docks. What did it matter to her if Kel ended up getting caught?

But she couldn't. He might not see her as a stray, but they weren't so different.

Moving quickly, she caught Kel right as he bumped into the man from behind.

The man spun, quickly grabbing Kel's hand. This time, with the leather purse clutched in his hand, there would be no hiding the fact that the stray had stolen from the rich man.

Streaks of red ran up the man's face and he lifted Kel off the ground by his neck. Kel couldn't be all that heavy, but seeing him lifted with one arm still shocked her.

"You know what happens to thieves?" the man said. Carth realized that this wasn't the same man she'd been following. That man had a silk hat and embroidery that marked him as someone with money. The man now holding Kel had a plain brown wool cloak and hard black eyes that reminded her of Felyn.

Kel tried kicking to get away, but the man held him. Kel's face went from red to blue and his eyes watered, tears streaming down his cheeks.

Carth froze. People gave space around them, not looking at the man, or if they did, they quickly glanced away. The man continued to squeeze, swinging Kel slightly until he stopped kicking and thrashing, until he almost stopped moving altogether. Another minute more and he'd be dead.

The man stared at Kel, saying nothing more. It was that empty expression that bothered her most, one that made it seem like killing Kel meant no more to him than stepping on a beetle. The same kind of expression that Felyn had had when he'd killed the A'ras.

Her mind went blank.

Carth darted forward, pulling the knife from her pocket as she did.

She moved quickly and silently and stabbed the man in the arm before slicing up at him.

With the first stab, he dropped Kel so that he lay in a heap on the ground, unmoving. The man managed to block the second swipe, ducking back. His eyes narrowed and he glanced at his arm a moment before looking at the knife Carth clutched.

She worried that he might attack her. If he was strong enough to lift Kel like that, then he would be strong enough to easily outmuscle her. But he didn't.

He took an unsteady step back.

Carth pushed on Kel with her foot, still holding the knife out. Kel rolled over, barely moving. "Get up!" she hissed.

He took a wheezing breath in and she glanced down for the briefest moment before turning her attention back to the man, but he was gone.

Carth held the knife out, her hand shaking as she did, afraid to put it back into her pocket in case the other man returned, but as people began filling the street around her again, she decided that he wouldn't return.

Kel moaned softly.

"Can you stand up?" she asked.

He opened his eyes. "What happened?"

She stuffed the knife back into her pocket, looking him over. Other than the red marking on his neck where she could practically trace the outline of the man's hand, he appeared unharmed. Color had returned to his face, though he now had a washed-out, sickly color to his skin. "You about got yourself killed, that's what happened."

Kel swallowed, and a pained look came to his face. "I remember that. How is it that you stopped it?"

"I'm not without skills."

He sat slowly and rubbed his neck, wincing as he did. "I feel like I've had my head in a noose."

"Not your head, but your neck at least."

Kel attempted to glare at her, but the anger faded. "Thanks."

She offered her hand and helped him to stand. "You wouldn't have needed help if you hadn't gone after him. Besides, that wasn't the same target as before."

"You're right. You were after him first. I should have left him… what do you mean it wasn't the same man?"

Now that he was standing, she wanted to get away from this place, away from where Kel had nearly been choked to death in the open, away from where no one had been even willing to help. The docks might not be the cleanest part of the city, but the people there had something of a code. She couldn't imagine a man simply killing a boy with others watching, unwilling to do anything.

"The man I tracked had a silk hat and embroidery. The man who nearly…"

"Killed me?"

She nodded. "His clothes were different."

A troubled expression passed over Kel's face. "I thought he was the same one. I was watching his back and never lost sight of him."

"You must have," Carth said.

They reached a busier section of the city, and the cawing of a gull made her feel more comfortable, knowing that they neared the docks. Wind gusted, carrying the stink of fish and grease, but she breathed them in, letting her heart begin to slow.

"I didn't think I had. I know how to collect scraps, Carth," he said, lowering his voice. "At least, I thought I did." He sighed, rubbing his neck.

The red mark where the man had gripped him had already purpled. It would turn into an ugly bruise and would take days to fade completely. How would they explain that to Vera? It had been bad enough trying to come up with an excuse about why they'd returned to the tavern sopping wet, and that after what had happened the night before. Now this? Vera would know something was up.

"You're going to have to cover that." She pointed to his neck and he jerked his head back and away. Carth's expression soured. "I wasn't going to touch it, but you're already bruising."

He touched the skin gingerly. "I know that."

"Then find a way to keep it covered up before we get back to the Lyre."

Kel wrapped his hand around his neck, only partially obscuring the markings. The man's hand had been enormous compared to Kel's neck. "How can I do that? It's not like I can wear a scarf all day."

Not a scarf, though some wore them in Nyaesh. Anything with too much color risked the appearance of affiliation with the A'ras, and unless you were a part of them, doing so would only get you hurt. "There might be some paints I could try," Carth said.

"Paint?"

"Oils," she said. "My mother once showed me—" She caught herself before sharing too much about her past. She'd made a point of not telling Kel and Etan about her family, not wanting to reveal anything more about herself than necessary. Why would she make that mistake now?

"What did your mother show you?"

She swallowed, wishing that she could have been more careful, but Kel didn't seem interested in asking about her mother, only about what Carth could do to help him hide the markings on his neck. "Different combinations of leaves and oils that create different colors."

"Will it work?"

Carth shrugged. If she managed to remember what her mother had taught her, and if she could mix it in the right way, she might be able to help paint over the skin enough for it to blend in. She wasn't sure how long it would last, but what did they have to lose?

"It might." She led him off Torrow Street and veered toward an herbalist that she knew of. When they stopped outside the door, she patted her pockets. "All I have are the scraps I collected earlier. How much do you have?"

Kel shook his head as he reached into his pocket. "Nothing more than a few coins."

He dropped three copper nils into her hand. Not enough for much, but the two silver vens she found in the purse she'd snared this morning might help. Carth didn't really know how much stuff like that cost. Her mother had had an interest in herbs and leaves and oils like that, but Carth had never taken much time to learn why. She'd watched her mother, though, and knew some of the more common combinations, even if she didn't know quite what they did.

"Hope this is enough," she said, mostly to herself.

She entered the shop and a soft tinkling sounded above the door, reminding her of the sound she'd heard when entering the temple. Carth froze for a moment, staring up at the door, wondering if this was a mistake. She wanted to help Kel, but if Vera discovered that they were deceiving her, how would she react? That might be worse than admitting what happened.

Kel bumped into her and she started forward.

Inside the shop were rows of bins. Each bin held different items: dried leaves, various lengths of branches, a few strange-smelling fruits, nuts from tiny to almost as large as her fist, and even a whole plant. Kel patted her arm and pointed to a wall where rows of jars held different-colored oils. Most had labels written in a tight scrawl, but not all; some had no label at all. A shelf near the front of the shop had rows of powders. Carth lifted the nearest one and opened the lid, and sniffed. A putrid odor hit her nose and she closed it quickly.

"This isn't a place for children."

Carth looked up to see an older woman with rheumy eyes and crooked hands tapping on the counter. She appeared so frail that it seemed like a gust of wind coming off the river would blow her away.

"We're looking for nevern oil and choclem leaves," Carth said quickly. They were two that her mother had used before when Carth had wanted something to paint.

"You are, are you?" the woman asked. She leaned on the counter, fixing Carth with her glazed eyes. "What do you think to do with such a combination? Nevern doesn't activate choclem. No point in mixing the two unless you wanted colorants…"

Her eyes drifted past Carth and settled on Kel. He slowly raised his hand to cover his neck, but not before the shopkeeper's mouth pulled into a tight line. "Colorant is what you want from it, isn't it?"

Lying to this woman would do no good, and it didn't really matter. Carth likely wouldn't see her again. She'd chosen this herbalist only because she knew how to find it, but there were others within the city, most nearer to where Carth had once lived. "That's what we need."

The old woman came around the counter and reached for Kel's neck. "Choclem will be too dark for his skin."

"What do you suggest?"

The herbalist turned to the shelf with the powders. "Depends on how long you intend the staining to last, and whether you wish to see other effects."

"It needs to last long enough that it won't be noticed." Carth frowned. "And what other effects?"

The herbalist set down one of the canisters without opening it and looked over her shoulder to Carth. "What other effects? Most who come here think that these leaves and oils have magical properties! Don't you want to see if you can heal your friend, maybe make him stronger, or richer, or—"

"I don't believe there's magic in your leaves."

The old woman chuckled. "No. That's not where the magic lives, now, is it?" She lifted a jar from the bottom shelf and went to the jars lining the wall, picking one with a slightly opaque color. She carried them toward the front of the shop and set them on the counter.

Carth watched as she pulled a small ceramic bowl from beneath the counter and tipped the nevern oil carefully into it, letting it drip slowly, almost as if she counted each individual drop. When satisfied, she opened the canister and used a long nail on her first finger to scoop a heap of the powder out before stirring it into the oil. The oil gradually darkened, thickening as it did. The woman touched it to her finger and pursed her lips in a frown. She took another smaller scoop of the powder and added this to the rest, stirring it until it mixed completely in.

"Try this," the woman said.

Carth touched her finger to the oil and found it stickier than she remembered nevern oil having been. She motioned for Kel to come to her and smeared it liberally around his neck, covering the angry purple bruise.

"It... burns."

"Of course it burns, boy. You're using nevern oil. It's painful at first, but that's how it gets beneath the surface. This should keep for nearly three days before you have to reapply. Not sure how long a mark like that will remain, but probably a week or two."

Carth realized that she didn't have anything to store the oil in.

The older woman seemed to realize it as well. She tapped the side of the bowl and disappeared into a part of the shop where Carth couldn't easily see her for a moment before reappearing carrying a small glass vial with a thick hunk of wax for a seal. "This should take care of you."

Carth took the vial with a cautious smile. "How much will we owe you?"

"For the nevern and vashi leaf? I think a copper is plenty. For the vial? Another copper."

Carth blinked. That was much less than what she would have expected. She slid the two copper nils that Kel had given her across the counter. "Thank you."

"No thanks. If you bring the vial back when you're done, I'll give you the copper back. It don't look to me like the two of you have all that much to spare."

Carth glanced at Kel. "Thanks," she said again.

The herbalist nodded and hobbled back into her shop, disappearing.

Carth grabbed Kel by the arm, not wanting to remain any longer than was necessary, and pulled him from the shop. Back in the sunlight, she examined the effect the oil had on Kel's neck. It wasn't perfect—if she stared closely at his skin, she could see that something wasn't quite right— but it was much less noticeable than it had been. And in the light of the tavern, it was likely that Vera wouldn't even notice.

"How does it look?"

Carth glanced over to the herbalist and found her watching through her window, staring out at them. "I think it will work well."

Kel smiled. "I can't believe it was only a copper!"

Carth couldn't either. There had to be something that they were missing, only she didn't know what that would be. As they made their way from the herbalist, a sense of longing lingered within her, one that reminded her of a simpler time, one of travels and games and a time when she didn't need to fear for her safety or worry about her friend. Seeing the herbalist left her wondering what would become of her now. How long could she stay with Vera and Hal? Not indefinitely, but where would she go?

Chapter 9

The stain faded by the middle of the third day. It happened quickly, almost as if the oil holding the vashi leaf powder simply stopped working. Had Carth not been watching Kel as he searched for scraps near one of the other taverns along River Street, she doubted that she would have noticed. As it was, she hurried over to him and tapped him on the shoulder.

"Your neck."

Kel stared ahead, watching a woman carrying a stack of fabric. Could the fool really think to take scraps from a shop owner? More than anything else, if he was discovered, Vera would definitely throw him out.

"What about it?" he asked absently. He moved forward, ignoring the way that she followed him.

"The oil has faded."

Carth touched the side of his neck and Kel jerked his head back and winced. Now that the oil had disappeared, it was clear that the bruising was still there. Not quite as purple, but it still appeared angry and hadn't seemed to fade nearly as much as Carth would have expected by now. Had Kel been more badly hurt than she had realized?

"Careful!"

"I didn't know it was still bothering you."

"It's not a bother," he said.

Carth pulled the vial of oil from her pocket and shook it. "You need to use this again."

Kel watched the woman hungrily, as if he intended to take her stack of fabrics from her, before turning back to Carth. "Get it over with."

She unstoppered the bottle and dabbed her finger to the surface. The oil had the same sticky consistency that she'd noted before, and she smeared it along his neck, quickly covering the bruising.

Kel clenched his jaw, breathing out with a soft groan. "It burns."

"I'm sorry. You need to use this."

"I might need to use it, but that doesn't mean I have to like it."

When Carth finished, she brought the oil-coated finger to her nose. Nevern oil didn't have much of an odor, but the vashi leaves powdered and mixed into the oil had a sharp, almost hot, scent to them.

"You done?" he asked.

Carth stuffed the wax back into the bottle. There wasn't much of the oil remaining—enough to coat him one more time, then she'd have to return to the herbalist for more. She doubted that would be a problem—the last few days she'd found herself drawn toward the herbalist shop. She could abandon the desire for vengeance and ask the old woman to let her apprentice. Carth figured she'd learned enough from her mother to make her useful. Once, she'd even thought she saw the woman watching before Carth scurried off, drifting back into the shadows of the street, always to return here.

"It's done. You don't have to act like I tortured you."

"Who's acting?"

Carth pushed him away, scanning the street for her next target. At midday, finding someone could be difficult. There were always plenty of people out in the streets, but often they were not the kind of people that she felt comfortable taking scraps from. Unlike Kel, she wasn't willing to go after shop owners, or even other women.

The longer she did this, the more she began to question whether she should. This wasn't the reason she remained here. She might not have a place to stay otherwise, but shouldn't she use her time to find a way to get revenge?

Kel locked eyes on someone and started away from her without a word. Carth watched, worried that he'd do something stupid again. He'd already nearly gotten caught twice, and both times he had needed her help in getting free. What would happen if she weren't there?

She heard the footsteps approaching and didn't need to turn to recognize Etan. He leaned in and spoke into her ear with a hot breath.

"I saw what you did with him."

Spinning, she jabbed at Etan with her finger. A part of her wished she could poke at him with her knife. "And what did I do with him?"

"What happened to Kel?" Etan asked.

"I don't know what you mean."

Etan sniffed. "I think you know exactly what I mean. You've got something in your pocket." He made a play to grab at her, but she was quicker than him and danced back and away from his attempt to grab at her pocket. "I'll find out what it is."

"You couldn't reach me if you wanted to," Carth said.

Etan's face contorted, twisting in an angry mask. "Careful, or you might find yourself woken in ways that you don't care for."

Carth thought about pulling the knife out of her pocket and jabbing it at Etan, but that wouldn't do anything but inspire him to pick on her more. She had enough trouble with him already; she didn't need to motivate him to do anything more.

"What do you think you can do?" she dared him.

Etan grabbed for her arm, but Carth backed away, slipping into the crowd.

She expected him to leave her, thinking that she would have to deal with him later, but he surprised her and gave chase, wearing a determined and satisfied look on his face.

Carth weaved between the crowd, getting as far from him as she could. She didn't fear Etan catching her here. That wasn't anything that he would do. No, she feared him attempting something while she slept. But she didn't want to let him catch her now.

She moved quickly, sticking to the sides of the streets, knowing ways to hide that she doubted he had discovered, keeping along the buildings, where she wouldn't have to work so hard to avoid running into people in the street. She put space between her and him as she worked her way up Doland Street. When she paused, she noted that he still chased her, hurrying up the street, unmindful of crashing into others as he did.

No... that wasn't what he did. The fool thought to bump and steal as he chased her! All it would take would be crashing into the wrong person, making the wrong lift, much like what Kel had experienced. She would have no interest in trying to help him if he did, not after the way that he'd been treating her.

She turned a corner, not wanting to watch.

The street was emptier than most, and darkened by the height of the buildings so that the sunlight didn't quite reach, leaving shadows stretching long across the cobbles. Carth moved quickly, trying to get as far away from Etan as was possible, but curiosity made her hesitate.

She turned back toward Doland Street.

As she did, she caught sight of a flash of maroon on a pair of men marching toward the docks.

A'ras.

They were rarely seen down by the docks. They came from time to time, but not as often as they patrolled in the rest of the city.

Slipping to the end of the street, she stood at the intersection, watching the A'ras as they made their way toward River Road. She saw no sign of Etan. At least he had the presence of mind to get out of the street when the A'ras came through. Risking their wrath meant certain imprisonment.

There came a soft scream.

Carth started forward, cursing herself. What was she doing risking herself against the A'ras? If they noticed her, they would have no reason not to pull her to them. And if they noticed her and realized that she carried one of their knives… that probably meant death.

There came another scream.

Damn the A'ras!

After what they had done to her family, a part of her wished that she had the same skill as Felyn, able to kill them with barely more effort than taking a stroll. All she had was her knife and the ability to move quietly. Maybe that was the real reason that her parents had taught her how to move quietly, to track without being seen, and to notice if someone followed. That would be a better reason than becoming the thief that she was.

She nearly reached River Road when she found the body.

An older man with dark hair much like her father's lay on the road, his neck split, and warm blood still pouring out onto the stones. He didn't move. Carth examined him, reaching into his pockets by instinct, and found a small purse that she pocketed. A slender knife rested under his arm.

Had this man thought to attack the A'ras?

What kind of fool thing was happening here? Were they finally coming after the Thevers? In the time she'd been on the docks, the Thevers hadn't bothered her at all, but she knew the A'ras intended to push them from the city.

Carth heard another shout.

She spun, twisting back toward the shadows of the nearest building, not wanting to be so easily seen in the street when the A'ras were out.

Nothing moved.

Where had Etan gone?

She should have passed him as she made her way down the street, unless he had veered off through one of the alleys, but she didn't think he had sense enough for that. Etan would have turned and run, not even smart enough to make an effort of hiding himself as he did.

Carth crept along the edge of the building, now holding onto the A'ras knife. The streets were silent, which troubled her more than anything. There should be noise of some sort: voices, or running, or even the steady rush of water along the rocks. Carth heard nothing.

She stopped at the corner. In the distance, she saw the sign for the Wounded Lyre, flapping in the steady breeze. The door to the tavern remained open.

Vera would never have left the door open.

Carth almost started forward when she saw a flicker of movement.

Near the opposite end of the street, it seemed as if shadows moved, almost as if they were alive.

Carth backed along the street again, afraid to move too far into the light. Whatever was out there made her nervous for reasons that she didn't understand.

Where had the A'ras gone?

She peeked her head around the corner, staying low to

the ground, and saw another flicker of shadow come, but this time closer.

Steel clanged on steel.

Unable to help herself, she stood, looking around the corner.

One of the A'ras had his sword unsheathed and battled something she couldn't see from her vantage. The A'ras moved quickly, and with deadly speed, but a dozen cuts lined his arms and his chest, telling Carth that he didn't move quickly enough, not for what he faced.

Not the Thevers. They were an ordinary sort.

Could that be Felyn?

He was the only person she'd ever seen move that quickly. No one else had the skill to withstand the A'ras. That was the reason they were so feared.

The fight shifted as another of the A'ras joined.

They danced down the street, moving away from the shops and toward the rocks, and then around a bend, until they were no longer visible.

Carth let out a shuddering breath.

What had she just witnessed?

People gradually came back out onto the street. Most looked around hesitantly, as if they were uncertain whether it was safe to return. A few hurried away from the docks, reaching Doland Street and passing her quickly as they raced away from the river.

Carth made her way toward the tavern. The door remained open, and no one had emerged from it. A nervous sensation in her stomach brought her forward, though there should be no reason for it. If the A'ras remained, the street would still have been empty. That it wasn't should reassure her.

At the door to the tavern, Carth hesitated. She rarely came into the tavern during the day. The daytime was for selling Vera's wares, or collecting scraps, not for sitting around inside while Vera baked and prepared for the evening rush. Hal ran errands, purchasing supplies, rolling barrels of ale and casks of wine from his suppliers or sourcing meats and flour and other ingredients that Vera needed to manage the tavern.

Inside, nothing moved.

Her heart fluttered a little faster.

She stepped inside, pulling the door closed behind her.

Carth scanned the tavern, but there was no one here. At this time of day, there should be a few people, at least. Staying along the wall, one hand still gripping her knife, she made her way to the kitchen. The door to the kitchen remained closed, and the small window was too high for her to easily peer into.

Taking a deep breath, she pushed the door open.

Vera stood next to the oven, kneading a thick roll of dough.

Tension left Carth's shoulders and she breathed out in a sigh.

Vera glanced over. "You're here early, girl. You done selling already?" she asked, eyeing Carth's empty hands.

Carth swallowed. One of these days, she feared Vera would discover that she didn't try to sell her breads or crafts for much. "Not yet. I... I was just checking that you were okay."

Vera leaned forward on the dough, pressing it flat with her large hands, resting her weight on it. "Why would you be worried about me?"

Carth glanced toward the tavern. "There's no one here."

Vera's eyes narrowed. "Hal was out there just a bit ago, girl. There were a handful of customers, enough to keep me busy when I should be getting my preparations ready for tonight."

"Where would he have gone?"

"Hal? The gods only know where that one goes. Trust him to get into trouble."

Carth felt the uneasy feeling begin to return. Vera thought that Hal had still been in the tavern, and the door had been open after the A'ras came through. "Did they come in here?"

"Did who, girl? Are you feeling well? You're acting strange."

She licked her lips and swallowed. "The A'ras. Did they come in here?"

Vera paused in between flipping the dough over and slammed it onto the table. She stood upright, straightening her back, and blinked slowly. "Now why do you have to go and mention them here?"

"They were on the street. A pair of them were here."

Vera started around the counter and hurriedly pushed past Carth. She paused in the doorway between the tavern and the kitchen, glancing toward the back of the tavern, but

Carth didn't have to look to know that no one was there. The tavern was as empty as the first time she'd come here.

"Damn that man," Vera said softly.

She hurried across the tavern and reached the door. She opened it a crack and peered out, looking into the street.

Carth stood under her arm. Activity in the street had returned to normal, as if nothing had happened. Would the dead man still be lying on the street or would someone have moved him? There had been another scream, but she hadn't seen another body. Maybe there wasn't anything more to find.

Vera stepped into the tavern. "Do you know where the others are?"

Carth shook her head. "Etan ran off. He was chasing a man…" She stopped before telling Vera all the details. She didn't want to know *how* they got the money they did. "The last I saw Kel, he was heading down the street."

Toward where the A'ras had disappeared, she realized.

"Go see if you can find them and then get back here," Vera said. "I'm going to look for that fool Hal."

As Vera started away, Carth said, "Vera?"

"What is it, girl?"

"Are you… are you worried for him?"

Vera sighed. "When it comes to *them*, I'm always worried."

Chapter 10

Carth made her way along the street, for once not bothering to try and hide, or to slink along as if she intended to collect scraps from someone. The A'ras might be gone, and people might have returned to the streets, but that didn't mean there wasn't tension about. Most people she passed were relatively silent and there was a somber air.

She found no evidence of the A'ras and whoever—or *whatever*—they had battled.

Where were Kel and Etan?

They could be anywhere along the riverfront. Normally she didn't fret about finding them, but then, she would often wander on her own for most of the day. Now that she *wanted* to reach them, she wouldn't be able to.

As she passed a low warehouse near the docks, she heard a voice she recognized, and paused. It was the man from the night she'd jumped into the river to save Kel.

"They grow bold," he said.

"As we knew they would." This other voice was lower and had a strange accent to the words.

"They travel freely now."

"They have done the same elsewhere for years."

Carth moved along the edge of the warehouse until she could see the cloaked form of the man from that night. In the daylight, he appeared nondescript: average height, short brown hair, a plain face, and a build that wouldn't stand out anywhere. Once again, he looked out over the river, as if expecting someone to come through here.

"Perhaps. But they have remained in the shadows here. That they should oppose the A'ras so openly means—"

"That they seek power. We have known that they would."

"If they acquire this power, they will be difficult to stop."

The other man sniffed. Carth still couldn't see him, but from the sound of him, he was close, likely right around the corner. "They were always going to be difficult to stop."

The visible man laughed softly. "You thought to use them, didn't you?"

"I have thought a great many things. In this land, many of them have gone awry."

"I don't understand."

"You no longer have to. That asset is gone."

"Asset. Is that all they were?"

"By choice, Jhon, do not think otherwise."

Carth took a step back.

Jhon.

It had to be more than a coincidence, didn't it? She remembered that name from the night her parents died. She hadn't seen him, but he had been in the temple with the man Ander.

How was it that she had come across him again?

Not only once, but repeatedly.

Did he know that she had been there?

How could they have known? She had been hidden in the temple, and they wouldn't have known that she had ended up with Vera and Hal... would they?

That wouldn't have been possible. Carth had ended up down by the docks purely by chance, not because she had chosen to come or had been guided here.

She took a step back and her foot slipped on the stone, making too much sound.

Carth was immediately aware of the noise. Her parents had taught her to pay attention to the sounds that she made, and this would have been noticeable.

She froze, heart racing and a cold sweat coming to her brow. If they *had* somehow managed to follow her, she couldn't risk them discovering her here, listening to them. Already she'd seen Jhon too often.

But had he wanted to harm her, wouldn't he have done so the last time he'd seen her? Unless he hadn't recognized her then.

If the other man was Ander, it was possible that they would recognize her this time.

She didn't want to risk it.

Moving carefully now, she made her way back to the street. She wasn't sure what she'd overheard, but whatever it was would be dangerous. They didn't fear the A'ras, not as they should—not as she did.

As she reached the street, she felt a firm tapping on her shoulder.

Carth turned, thinking that maybe Kel or Etan had found her, hopeful that they would be able to return to Vera's tavern and discover what had happened with Hal. Hopefully nothing.

Jhon stood in front of her, his plain face considering her with a neutral expression.

"Have you learned how to use your knife?" he asked.

Carth took a step back, glancing around for Ander. That had to be the other man she had overheard... unless it was the man from that night in the tavern, the one with the gold bracelet and the stack of coins. She didn't see him.

Instead, across the street, Kel started toward her. He wore a look of concern and had a gash along the side of his face. At least now he didn't need to fear hiding the bruising on his neck quite so much.

Carth shook her head and shot him a warning glance. She didn't need for him to get mixed up in whatever Jhon and Ander were up to, not any more than he already was. Bad enough that they had helped to rescue him when he'd nearly drowned.

"Now you won't talk?"

Carth pulled her focus back to him. "What do you want with me?"

A hint of a smile pulled at his mouth. As it did, he took on an air of something that was more than the plain-appearing man he otherwise seemed. "After pulling you from the river after you fell in, I didn't think that you would risk yourself again."

"I told you that I didn't fall in."

The smile pulled a little more and made him appear more youthful than he looked otherwise. When it faded, it became difficult to tell his age again. "That's right. You jumped in. After him." He nodded toward the other side of the street, where Kel attempted to hide, but was unsuccessful.

"That's right. He was the one who fell in."

"How was it that he did? He doesn't appear all that clumsy, but then I haven't watched him quite as much as I've been watching you."

Carth swallowed. "You've been watching me?"

"It is difficult not to watch. I must say, you really are more skilled than your partners."

"They're not my partners."

"No?" He glanced over to Kel. "You're not related, and you are much too young to be anything more than friends. I would say that makes you partners. And not of the Thevers, or the A'ras would have come after you as well."

Carth flushed at the thought of anything more with Kel. The stupid boy had nearly died too many times to count. Were she not so willing to help him, he wouldn't still be alive. "We're not related, if that's what you're getting at."

"No. Were you related, he might have swifter hands. Lucky that he didn't suffer any more than he did, don't you think?"

"What is that supposed to mean?"

Jhon offered that half smile again, the one that made him look so much more youthful than he did when he didn't smile. "That means that he's lucky to have only that bruise you managed to cover up. I am interested in learning how you learned such a skill."

Carth looked over at Kel. From here, she could make out the faint traces of the oil that stained his neck. It gave him some color, but not enough to look completely natural. This application hadn't worked quite as well as the first.

"It wasn't me. There is an herbalist."

"Yes, I am aware that there are herbalists. How is it that you thought to visit one?"

"I… I saw someone use them before," she lied. Maybe he didn't know that she had been in the temple that night her parents had died. If not, then it was possible she could keep from him the fact that her mother had taught her about oils and leaves and other things like that.

"Is that right? What combination did you use?"

Carth considered whether she should even answer, but what could it hurt if she did? Worse, Jhon might have learned anyway. He had known about the bruising, which meant that either he had seen them after the attack, or he had witnessed Kel's attack… and Carth's response.

Was that the reason he'd questioned whether she had learned more about the knife? Did he do that to taunt her?

"Nevern oil and vashi leaves."

His eyes narrowed slightly. "That would color the flesh, but I suspect it burns a bit."

She glanced past him to Kel, who still hadn't moved. "He said it does."

"He did. Does it not burn you?"

Carth shrugged. "I didn't apply it to my skin."

"No, but I believe that you helped your… friend… apply

it. Did it have so little effect on you?"

"I barely touched it."

"But you touched it."

"What are you getting at?"

"Only that you are an interesting person. I have thought so since I first saw you."

Carth took a shallow breath to steady herself. "And when was that?"

"I thought we established that I pulled you from the water when you jumped in. Unless you think that we have met another time? Perhaps in the tavern, when you reconsidered stealing from my asset."

"Why was he your asset?"

"He provides me with information."

"Why?"

"Because I have asked him."

"Why do you want information?"

That half-smile returned. "There are many reasons to want information."

"Do you work with the A'ras?"

His face clouded for the briefest of moments. "There is no working *with* the A'ras." He said the word differently, so that it rolled off his tongue with a strange lilt.

"Then why do you need an asset?"

"Why do you steal?"

Carth was taken aback. "What kind of question is that?"

"I think that it's the same sort of question as the one you asked. In fact, mine might be less intrusive, as what you do could be considered offensive to the A'ras and the royal family. I believe the punishment were you caught stealing would be *quite* harsh."

Carth paled. "They would never do that to someone my age." That had been the reason Etan claimed that the strays could get away with it. Were they any older—and really, Etan might still be in danger of it—they would run the risk of losing a hand for stealing. Repeat offenders lost the other. And a third offense meant death.

"Are you certain? I can't say that I'm as familiar with the laws of Nyaesh as I am with others, but it seems to me that they don't have the same concerns with age as you would find in other places."

"You're not from Nyaesh?"

Jhon smiled again. "That was what you took away from what I said?"

She shrugged.

"No. I am not of Nyaesh. As you have seen, there are many not of this land who live here. Your coloring tells me that you were not originally from here, either. I would imagine that you are either of Al-shar or possibly Pey or even…" He frowned, studying her.

"Al-shar," she said quickly. Better to divert him from knowing where her parents actually came from. Not that it mattered. There weren't many who had heard of Ih-lash, so even were she to claim that she was from that distant land, it was unlikely that it would mean anything to him.

"Indeed? You must have been in Nyaesh for many years."

"Why?"

"You have no accent. And your hair…"

Carth hadn't considered whether she would actually look like someone from Al-shar. She knew almost nothing about the land, but it seemed to her that she should just as likely be from Al-shar as from Ih-lash.

"I have no memory other than Nyaesh," she said.

He nodded. "That would explain much. How old are you?"

"Twelve."

"A difficult age, especially when you live in this part of the city. I am surprised that your mistress allows you to wander so freely."

"My mistress?"

"At the Wounded Lyre, if I'm not mistaken. Most would expect a girl of your age to be working in the kitchen and learning the trade."

Vera hadn't shown any interest in working with Carth. Her mother had, but then her mother had shown her things that had no bearing on any sort of future role she might have. "I have been learning the trade," she said.

"Indeed? Is that why she has you here, risking yourself?"

"I'm—"

"You are collecting scraps, I believe is what you say, is it not?"

Carth looked past Jhon, wanting to get away from him, but there was no easy way around him, not without crashing into him. As compact as he might be, he still filled the street, managing to make himself appear larger. The hint of a smile, much less than what he'd displayed before, told her that he knew exactly what he did.

"What do you even know?" she demanded.

Jhon tilted his head. "Not as much as I would like to, I think. I have many questions when it comes to you, Carthenne Ih-thanor."

She sucked in a quick breath. He had known exactly where her family's homeland was, as well as her father's name. He had used the formal name, one that she had only heard spoken by those who knew Ih-lash as her parents had known it. How was it possible that he knew?

"What do you want with me?" she asked. Attempting to run or find a way to hide would do no good, not when there was someone who knew her the way he appeared to know her. She wanted to run, but where was there for her to go? She could run to the river and attempt to jump in, maybe swim down the shore, but the last time she had attempted that, it had not gone that well. The only thing she had that might help her escape if he tried to attack her was the A'ras knife.

"I want the same as you, I suspect. I would have answers."

"That's not what I want at all."

"Oh? What is it you would have?"

Carth blinked slowly. What would he know about what drove her? She didn't care if she ever understood. All she wanted was a way to obtain the revenge she sought for her parents.

"Ah," Jhon said, almost as if he understood her thoughts. "You want something that you cannot have, at least not in the form that you think. But if you find understanding, then you might learn."

While Jhon had been speaking to her, she noticed that Kel had been creeping forward. For the first time, he managed to move quietly enough that he didn't gain the attention of the other man. Carth tried to keep her gaze on Jhon, not wanting to draw attention to the fact that Kel approached.

"There are things that I could help you understand, Carthenne Ih-thanor. They are lessons your parents would have taught you had they only—"

Kel crashed into him, sending Jhon sprawling forward. The look of surprise—and, strangely, sadness—on his face caught her off guard. When he struck the ground, his head bounced off the cobbles. Jhon's eyes went closed and he didn't move.

"Blessed Assage! I didn't mean to kill him!" Kel swore.

Carth paused and searched Jhon's cloak. The man had been about to tell her something about her parents, and he *had* seemed to know something about her family. Had she misread the situation so much that she didn't understand why he had come to her in the first place? Could he really not want to harm her?

She tugged on her braid with one hand while she bit her lip, checking him with her free hand. A steady pulse beat within his chest. Carth leaned back on her heels, considering what she should do, when she heard the sound of thudding footsteps along the stones.

"Carth!" Kel urged. "We need to get moving."

He pulled on her arm. She wanted nothing more than to wait for Jhon to awaken, find out what he might have known about her parents. Had her parents taught her so that she could learn ways to avoid men like Jhon, or had there been another reason?

When she didn't move fast enough, Kel released her arm and raced to the street. When he came back to her, his eyes were wide and his face was as white as parchment. "We have to go. The A'ras... they're here."

Chapter 11

As Kel pulled her along the street, away from the downed form of Jhon, Carth couldn't shake the sense that she should find a way to wake him and drag him with her. Instead, as Kel pulled her away from the alley, she feared that she wouldn't find Jhon again, that something would happen to him and she would never find what he might have to tell her.

The footsteps grew louder.

Kel pulled on her with greater urgency. "Go on!" she told him.

"I'm not leaving you here. Not as *they* come."

Now he would find nobility?

She let him drag her down the street, but she kept her eyes on Jhon as she did. He still didn't move, not even to roll over or shift out of the way. If the A'ras came across him, what would happen?

It was possible that they would kill him.

Carth swore to herself and jerked on Kel's arm, breaking free of his grip.

"What are you doing?" he demanded.

"We can't leave him here."

Kel looked at her as if she had lost her mind, and Carth decided it was possible that she had. "What does it matter if they find him?"

Carth raced to Jhon, who still lay unmoving. "It matters."

She grabbed him by the legs and tried dragging him. Jhon wasn't a large man, but then, she wasn't a strong girl, either. He didn't budge no matter how hard she tried.

She looked up at Kel as he hurried over to her. "You'll have to help me."

"Help? Are you *mad*?"

The sound of voices came near, and with it came the steady sensation of sizzling in her skin—like a burning below the surface that pulsed in her veins—that she attributed to magic being used. There was no doubting that the A'ras were near now. "Yes. I am mad. Now help me!"

Kel stared at her for another moment before shaking himself. He grabbed one of Jhon's legs and helped Carth pull on him, dragging him along the stones. He moved slowly and thudded against the cobbles, likely making enough noise that anyone listening from the street would hear them. When Kel grunted softly with his effort, she shot him a warning glance and he only shook his head.

They reached the back side of the warehouse. A stack of crates leaned against the building, nearly as high as both of them, but barely wide enough to hide them all.

The sound of the A'ras voices drew nearer.

"Hurry!" she whispered.

Kel leaned forward and his eyes went wide. "What do you think I'm doing?"

They dragged Jhon behind the crates just as the footsteps rounded the back of the warehouse.

Carth pulled the knife from her pocket and held it in front of her.

Kel studied the knife as if seeing it for the first time, which he was, she realized. When she'd jabbed at him, it had been at night. The only other time she'd pulled the knife out around him had been when that strange man had been choking him.

He opened his mouth to say something, but she raised a finger to her lips to motion him to silence.

"There is something here," a voice said. The A'ras speaking had a strange and harsh voice, making it sound as if he spoke through a thickened tongue. "I can sense it."

"You sense nothing," another voice said. "Almars warned us to watch for signs of Reshian, but we would not find anything back here."

The other A'ras seemed to sniff at the air, and then inhaled deeply. "I'm not so sure that there isn't," he said. "Listen to what the water tells you, and the air."

The other A'ras chuckled softly, a dark sound that easily carried behind the stacked crates. Carth shivered.

"You've listened to Invar too much if you think there are lessons that could be learned from the water and the air."

"I listen when there are things that can be learned. You would be wise to do the same."

The steady sizzling sensation came again, this time searing

through her skin, leaving her flesh feeling dry and tight. She'd only ever felt the same around the A'ras and knew that it came when they used their magic. It was that magic that made her fear the easy way Felyn had managed to destroy the three A'ras. If he could do that so easily against men charged with power, there was little anyone else would be able to do against him.

"As I said, there's nothing here," the other A'ras said.

"Hmm. I'm unconvinced."

A crack echoed through the air. "You don't have to be convinced. Come on. We're getting called."

Carth heard the sound of feet moving quickly over the cobbles away from her. Kel started to move away from the crate, but she grabbed his arm, holding him in place even when he shot her a questioning glance. She held a hand up.

A rustling sound came from nearby. Likely fabric, and it was close.

Kel gave her a beseeching stare, but she didn't know what to do.

Then Jhon began to move.

That was the last thing that they needed. He couldn't wake up and make noise, not if there was one of the A'ras nearby. Carth didn't harbor any hope that she would be able to do anything were the A'ras to find her. It was one thing to stab some random man on the street when he had a friend hung up by his neck, but it was quite another to stab one of the magically empowered servants of the royals.

The rustling came even closer.

Another moment, maybe two, and they would be discovered.

She held the knife out, ready to do whatever it took to keep them safe but knowing that there wouldn't really be anything that she could do if the A'ras came around the stack of crates.

Another crack shook the air.

Carth tensed and noted that Kel did the same. She shook her head when he looked over at her. How much longer would they be able to hide here?

The shuffling started to move away.

Carth still didn't move, clutching the knife tightly in her hand. She didn't dare do anything else but hold on to the knife, but if the A'ras saw her with it, there would be no question what fate would await her, and it would be much worse than if she were caught stealing.

Then the sound of the A'ras made its way around the corner of the warehouse and finally disappeared.

She allowed herself to breathe out, finally able to relax.

Jhon stirred more, but still hadn't woken.

Kel grabbed onto her arm and she nodded. Now it was time to go, and to return to the Lyre if they couldn't find Etan first. Staying out on the street was dangerous.

As they cleared the crates, she thought she heard Jhon beginning to sit. Carth didn't slow, and she refused to go back to ask the questions that she so badly wanted to ask, fear of remaining on the street overriding her desire for answers. Taking Kel's hand, she ran back to the tavern.

"Where is that fool man?" Vera stormed around the tavern, carrying a large ladle as if she might use it to smack the first person who refused to answer her. As there were only Carth and Kel in the tavern right now, both tensed as she came near, neither wanting her ladle to their head.

"We didn't see him," Carth said again.

"What did you see?" Vera asked as she stopped pacing, holding the ladle back over her shoulder. Carth eyed it, afraid that Vera might swing it down at her, even though Vera had never attacked her in the time she had stayed with her.

Carth glanced at Kel, warning him to silence. She didn't want Vera to know anything about Jhon and the fact that he knew something about her family. Those were questions that she would have to have answered eventually, but for now, the focus needed to be on what had happened to Hal.

"Two of the A'ras," Carth said.

Vera glared at her but didn't warn her to shush as she normally did. "They shouldn't even be down here," she said in a whisper.

"Why?"

Vera shook her head. "Doesn't matter."

Carth almost stood. "It does matter, especially if they come after us. We should know why they aren't supposed to be here, and how to avoid them. Besides, I thought they came after Thevers down here."

"Carth—" Kel said.

"The girl is right," Vera said with a sigh. "They're mostly paid to stay clear."

"Paid?"

Vera nodded.

"But why? To protect the Thevers?"

"That's why some do it, but not why we do."

"I... I don't even understand! How do you have enough to keep them..." Her mind raced and she understood what had happened, and how Vera would have managed to keep the A'ras away. "That's why we sell breads and crafts, isn't it?"

Vera sighed. "That's part of it. Business is enough that we have extra, but what you bring in helps." She smiled warmly at them, and Carth felt a flush rising within her at the deception. "They leave us alone, even with the obsession about—" She shook her head, as if thinking better about sharing. "We're buying protection, not only for the Lyre, but for the other shops along the riverfront."

"Did you miss a payment?" Kel asked.

"They wouldn't let me miss anything," Vera said.

"Why did they come down here, then?" Carth asked. She hadn't realized it before now, but in the time she'd been with Vera and Hal, she *hadn't* seen any of the A'ras down near the river other than that first day. They were much more prevalent in other parts of the city, and practically impossible to avoid in certain places.

"I don't know," Vera said.

"They were looking for something," Kel said. "We heard them."

"You heard them?" Vera asked.

Kel nodded. "Carth hid us until they went away."

"The A'ras do not simply go away," Vera said. "That is why they are so effective for the royal family. When they don't find what they search for, they will stay on the hunt until they find it."

Carth shivered. Had they hunted for her? Or had they hunted for Jhon? Either way, now that she had been responsible for hiding from them, would they come after her?

Vera watched Carth and seemed as if she wanted to say something, but she didn't get the chance to do so.

The door to the tavern opened and Hal entered, carrying a small child. Vera let out a relieved sigh and ran over to him, lifting the child from him. "Haldon Marchon! Where have you been?"

"Found another stray," he said.

"You found this one?" Vera asked.

"Found. Delivered to me. What does it matter? They need our help and we have to give it to them."

Vera glanced at Carth and Kel. "It matters, I think. More than ever, I think that it matters."

Hal stiffened, as if noticing the mood in the tavern for the first time. "What happened?"

Vera pulled the child over to the fire and set him down on a stool. Carth noted bruising along the child's face and a deep wound on the back of his head. Vera wasted no time putting pressure on the wound and beginning to clean it.

"They came here," Vera said.

Hal glanced at Carth. "They should not have. That's why we pay them."

"That was why we had paid them," Vera said.

Hal slowly looked over at Vera. Something passed

between them, and Carth could tell that it was important but didn't know what it might be.

"Come, the two of you," Hal said. He motioned for them to follow as he left the tavern, and then stopped, turning to them and blocking off Carth's view of the rest of the street. "Tell me what you remember."

Kel spoke first, sharing what he had seen of Jhon as he had trapped Carth in the alley. How much had he overheard? It couldn't have been that much or Kel would not have intervened, but enough that he recognized her concern about the fact that he'd found her.

Hal watched her, saying nothing at first.

When Kel was done, Hal shifted his attention to her. "What happened, Carth?"

"I don't know."

"Hmm. There would be a reason that they would focus on you, I think."

Kel looked at her and must have seen the terror on her face. She didn't want to explain what had happened to her parents, or why she had run from the A'ras, or even why she would know Jhon. She didn't want to share with either of them that she would do anything to get revenge for what happened to her mother—to both her parents, but she hadn't *seen* what had happened with her father—even if that meant attacking the A'ras.

"They weren't looking for me," she said.

"Then what were they looking for?" Hal asked.

"I don't know. Someone else."

Vera hollered for Hal. He sighed and turned toward the

tavern. "If you've caught their attention, there might not be anything we can do to protect you."

"They're not after me," Carth said again.

Hal watched her for another moment before nodding and entering the tavern once more, leaving Carth alone with Kel.

"I heard him," Kel said.

"Yeah? I heard Hal too," Carth said.

"That's not what I'm talking about."

Carth tried to move past Kel, but he moved to block her. He wasn't large, but then neither was she, and she didn't want to push past him, not with what he'd been through over the last day or so. "Get out of the way," she said.

"What was he talking about to you? Something that man said bothered you. That was the reason you didn't want to leave him for the... for *them*."

"It's nothing."

"Nothing? We could have been killed because you wanted to keep him from getting killed."

"We weren't in any real danger," Carth said, though she didn't believe it. Had the A'ras found them, there wasn't any telling what he might have done to them, but hiding Jhon—whoever he was—while she had one of their knives would have been a sure way of getting all of them hurt.

"You're not going to say anything more?" Kel asked.

"What do you want me to say?" Carth asked. "That I watched as my mother was killed by someone who killed *them* without any more concern than you would have for swatting a fly? That the man you knocked out seemed to know something about my family and about what had happened, so that I could finally get answers? Is that what you wanted to hear?"

Kel took a step back, looking as if he had been slapped. "I didn't know."

Tears welled in her eyes and Carth stormed away rather than let Kel see her crying. She didn't need him or Etan to tease her any more than they already did. "I know. You've been more concerned about whether I was a real stray. And maybe I'm not, but that doesn't mean that I have anyplace else to go!"

She ran down the street, hiding her eyes, wanting to get as far away from him as possible.

Chapter 12

For the first few days after she had protected Jhon, the relationship between Carth and Kel and Etan grew even more strained. As much as she wanted to repair that connection, she struggled. Something had changed for Kel that night, much like something had changed for her.

The small boy Hal brought in stayed on the top bunk. Stiv was the first stray Hal had brought to them since Carth's arrival. Etan made a point of tormenting him, much as he had tormented Carth during her first days. She wondered if he had done the same with Kel, though the two of them seemed to have something of a friendship now, even if they had not always. Would she develop the same with Etan over time? The longer she knew him, the less likely it seemed. More and more, Etan seemed mostly interested in disappearing during the day, leaving her and Kel alone.

Even with Kel, Carth remained alone. No longer did he stand along the shadows of the street, watching for targets. He preferred to keep a distance, as if seeing Carth's willingness to help Jhon had changed something for them.

Worse was that Vera and Hal seemed distant. They had welcomed her to the tavern and had given her a place to stay, but she no longer felt the same warmth from them. Vera never treated her any differently and willingly accepted the coins Carth offered, but her eyes wore a flat expression when before there had been depth.

Stiv followed Carth most days. She hadn't the heart to keep him from following her, and with Kel shutting her out, it was nice having someone with her. He wasn't a bother, not really, and his deep brown eyes watched her with a bright curiosity.

"Why do you keep sneaking away?" he asked her on the third day since he'd come to the Wounded Lyre.

It shouldn't be her explaining to him what was expected of him, should it? Kel or Etan did a better job and had been here longer. Etan had offered to work with Stiv, but the boy had so far avoided him. Kel and Etan stayed together as they often did, watching her from across the street.

"Doesn't matter," Carth said.

Stiv held up the sack Vera had given him. "Vera wants me to sell these sweetbreads."

Carth nodded. "Good luck."

"Is that what you do? Are you finding a better place to sell your breads?"

Carth glanced at Stiv. She didn't want to be the one to tell him how she managed to collect all the scraps she did. Let him remain untouched by the seedy side of the city. He didn't deserve whatever had made him a stray—none of them did. Let Stiv hold on to that innocence a little longer.

"That's what I do." She started away from him, not wanting to lie to him any more. It was bad enough that Kel and Etan had drawn her into their collections. She didn't want them to draw Stiv into it as well.

As she crossed the street, Stiv caught her and grabbed onto her arm. "How are you selling them? I haven't managed to sell any!"

Carth turned and faced him, leaning forward to meet his eyes. "Do what you have to to collect enough to keep yourself safe," she said.

Stiv blinked. "Safe from what?"

Carth glanced back at the tavern. From what? Not Vera and Hal. They had welcomed her when they didn't have to, and now they feared she'd brought the attention of the A'ras to their tavern.

"How did you end up here? Where did Hal find you?" she asked.

Stiv looked to the ground. "I don't want to talk about it."

Carth had assumed that Hal brought Stiv here to help him, but what if that wasn't the case? "Did he force you to come?" she asked.

"What? No!"

"Then where?"

Stiv swallowed. "My family... they're gone. Caught in the fighting."

"Why?"

Stiv frowned. "They're Reshian, like you."

"I'm not Reshian."

Stiv's eyes widened. "I'm sorry. I wasn't serious when I said that."

Carth sighed. "I'm not going to hurt you, Stiv. Just do your best to sell the breads. Otherwise you'll have to learn to collect scraps."

"Collect what?" Stiv asked.

She hadn't determined how old he was. Possibly eight, but he was skinny enough that he could pass for much younger. The clothes Hal had found for him were a few sizes too big. Mostly they looked to be Kel's castoffs. His wavy brown hair hung to his shoulders and had been matted until Vera had taken the time to wash it.

Carth pulled one of the coin purses that she'd snatched from well-dressed men from her pocket and shook it. "Coins."

His eyes widened as he stared at the coin pouch. "Where did you get that?"

She debated answering, but how could she keep that from Stiv? He was a stray, no different from her. "Either you sell breads or you collect scraps. That's what you need to learn. Either way, you bring what you get to Vera." And then she would use it to buy protection from the A'ras. Or had. Would it still work? Would they be safe from them?

"Scraps?"

She nodded. "You'll learn to collect enough. It's your way of thanking her and Hal for giving you a place to stay and a place to sleep."

Stiv reached for the purse. Carth let him have it. It was easier for her to collect coins than for him. "How am I supposed to do this?"

She wanted to teach him, to show him what he would need to do, but that wasn't why she was here. There were things she needed to learn, and that meant she had to find Jhon, discover what he knew about her family and how he seemed to know so much about her.

"Ask Kel. Or Etan. He's a little better than Kel anyway."

She nodded toward the other boys. They stood too openly, and when Kel lumbered toward the man he targeted, Carth could tell he wouldn't be able to hide himself as well as he needed. For someone who was supposed to collect scraps, the same person who had taught her, he did a poor job of it.

"What can they show me?" Stiv asked.

Carth grabbed Stiv by the shoulders and guided him across the street. She stood in the shadows between a pair of buildings, wanting nothing more than to hide. A cloud moved over the sun, giving her a bit more coverage as she watched. "See what he does?" Carth asked, pointing to Kel.

Stiv watched Kel, and his eyes widened when Kel bumped into the man and lifted a purse from his pocket. Kel immediately turned toward an alley and disappeared. The man took a few steps before patting his pocket and apparently realizing what had happened. With a shout, he turned and chased after Kel, but Carth knew he would be safe. He might not be clever with his hands, but he would be quick in the alleys.

"What did he do?" Carth asked.

Stiv looked up to her. "He... he *stole*."

Carth nodded. "Decide what you'll do. And don't tell

Vera. You don't have to collect scraps the same way Kel does. If you don't, then you sell the sweetbreads, make a few copper nils a day, and bring those to Vera." She shrugged. "If you do, and if you get lucky, then you can collect a bit more. Either way, you'll be safe."

"What happens if I don't make enough?"

"You will."

"But if I don't?"

Carth watched Etan standing on the side of the street, eyeing her and Stiv. "You'll be fine."

She patted him on the shoulders and left him.

Carth slipped along an alley, getting away from the docks and away from the noise, making her way through the city. She paused at the herbalist, tempted to return. Were she to learn an honest trade, wouldn't it be at a place like that? Her mother would have wanted her to learn. They were lessons that she had tried teaching her, but Carth had only been interested in playing games with her father. Because of that, both of her parents were gone.

The old woman in the shop must have been looking out the window. She pushed open the door and waved to Carth, motioning her into the shop.

"Have you come for more nevern oil and vashi leaves?"

Carth shook her head. She eyed the bins of branches before turning to the wall of oils. Even her mother would have been impressed with the variety. "What you gave us the last time was enough. Thank you."

"Gave? Who said I gave you?"

Carth bobbed her head and fished the vial out of her

pocket before handing it back to the woman. That must have been why she had wanted her to come back to the shop.

The old woman waved her hand. "I didn't really worry about that. I know enough craftsmen who can make me more."

Carth paused at the shelf with the leaves. Many were in jars, and powdered. She remembered going with her mother when she collected leaves, and her mother playing a game of asking the name of each leaf she collected, and then asking how best to store them. As much as Carth cared for her mother, she had no interest in herbalism. Her mother had never said it, but Carth suspected that disappointed her.

"How do you get so many different varieties?" She leaned forward, recognizing flatwort leaves. These were spotted with wide purple splotches, harvested when the flatwort would be the most potent.

"I collect them," the woman answered. "What herbalist does not collect her own supplies?"

"But you can't find flatwort anywhere around Nyaesh, and the goldenrod is much brighter than what you can find near here."

The woman stared at her with a funny expression. She lifted the jar containing the goldenrod leaves. They were a brilliant gold like their namesake, and the long, slender leaves rolled into a tube shape. The variety around the city had a much paler color, one that matched Stiv's hair.

"You know of goldenrod?"

Carth nodded absently as she moved along the shelf, looking at a few other items. "My mother would drag me along when she harvested leaves."

"Your mother is an herbalist?"

Carth glanced up. "I don't think she would call herself that. She had an interest." She shrugged. "She was always mixing concoctions for my father and me."

"Ah, I should have known you had some talent when you first came to my shop. Not many understand the different oils, particularly nevern oil." The herbalist smiled. "You don't sound as if you were impressed by what she makes for you."

"Made," Carth said. She was proud of herself that she didn't begin crying when speaking of her mother. It had taken her a long time to reach that point, but now she could think on her without the tears flowing, and without the painful knot forming in her throat, and without the gnawing in her belly that she'd once had.

The herbalist nodded. "She is gone, then."

"She is."

"Ah, so many lost these days, especially with what happens outside of the city."

Carth didn't know much about what happened outside the city. Her parents had protected her from it, but they had always moved her south.

"There are few who take an interest in such things," the herbalist went on. "Alchemists do. Herbalists such as myself. Healers understand that different plants and oils can be used in healing salves and medicines. I have not heard of too many with a passing interest." The herbalist slid the jar back onto the shelf and stopped at the counter, leaning on it. "Did she have a shop such as this?"

Carth shook her head. "I don't think she ever sold what she made. If she did, I never saw it."

The herbalist smiled, but this time it didn't reach all the way to her eyes. "You and your father were her only customers! Almost as if you had your own shop."

"My mother would take her powders as well," Carth said.

"Of course she would," the herbalist said. "All good practitioners do." The woman used the counter for support as she weaved around to the other side. "You have an eye for herbs, you know."

"I don't have an eye. I recognized the ones that my mother showed me."

"Interesting that she would teach you about flatwort."

Carth looked up from the row of dried fruit. Most were berries she recognized, though some were more exotic than anything that she would normally find in Nyaesh. Why hadn't she noticed that when she had been here the last time?

But then, she had been more concerned about Kel. She had wanted to do anything to help him mask the bruising, and disguise it so that Vera wouldn't see it and get upset. There hadn't been the time—or the interest—to wander through the herbalist's shop.

"Why is that interesting?" Carth tried to think about what she'd learned of flatwort, but those memories were hazy. She'd never *really* paid attention when her mother demonstrated the different leaves. When she would get going talking about them, Carth often started to lose focus, not paying the same attention to her mother as she gave to her father when he discussed strategies for following someone, or how he could climb onto rooftops.

"Oh, there are plenty of uses for flatwort, but unless you know what you're doing, the plant is dangerous. The leaves are similar to another—"

"Gardash," Carth said, the name coming to her.

The herbalist watched her a moment. "Yes. It is called that in some places. In Nyaesh, it is known as shadesbreath. A deadly plant, and one that is much too like flatwort for most. With flatwort, the leaves have three larger spots. With shadesbreath, they are smaller, but still three." She smiled. "The other differences are more difficult to detect."

Carth remembered her mother describing something about gardash. Wasn't it something about veins on the bottom of the plant? She couldn't remember.

"Worse, they grow in many of the same climates." The woman rustled behind her counter and pulled a jar out, which she set on the counter. Inside were leaves that looked no different than the flatwort that the woman had in the other jar. Carth doubted she would have been able to pick one out as different from the other.

"Why is gardash—shadesbreath—so dangerous?"

"Ah, because most die simply touching the leaves."

Carth glanced at the jar and wondered why the herbalist would even have such a thing here, especially if it was that dangerous. Did she *want* someone to accidentally grab the jar and get poisoned? "Most?"

"Not all would suffer. Like many things, there are those immune to that particular effect."

The herbalist shook the jar slightly and then set it back

under the counter. "Better not to pay much attention to things like that," she said. "Too many have suffered, especially here."

The way she said it made Carth wonder if shadesbreath was the reason that the A'ras blades were so dangerous. Did they use something like that to poison the blade? Probably not. Carth had touched the blade countless times and had never been harmed.

"Was there anything in particular that you wanted?" the herbalist asked.

Carth scanned the shop, looking around one more time before turning away. She had thought... no, there was nothing for her here. Her mother might have wanted her to know about leaves and plants, but she had never taken the time to understand them. And now... now she would never get to learn. Now she had become a thief.

"I'm sorry to have bothered you," she said.

The woman watched Carth for a moment, then smiled. "There is no bother. Come as often as you would like. It's always pleasant speaking to those with a shared interest."

Carth turned away without saying anything more. She didn't want to hurt the old woman's feelings by telling her that she had no interest. Had she any interest in learning from her mother, she might have something of a future. Instead, she was forced to use the skills her father had taught her, but there was only one way she could use his skills, which meant that she had no other destiny but to be a thief.

Did that mean that someday, the Thevers would expect her to join? Was *that* what she was meant to become?

Chapter 13

Days passed uneventfully. As much as Carth wanted to find Jhon and discover what he might know about her family, she feared what she might learn. What would she say if she learned that her father *had* been a thief of some sort? Realizing that he'd prepared her for it made her more concerned about the man he was, and in a way, she didn't want to know the truth.

She wondered how she had not seen it before, but she hadn't *wanted* to see it. Her father had been... well, he'd been the one person she'd looked up to. With him gone, she had no one.

With each day, she wandered the streets near the docks, hesitating to travel too far into the rest of the city. She didn't need to go beyond the docks to grab enough coin to appease Vera, and with Stiv wandering through the streets, still intent to sell Vera's sweetbreads, she preferred to keep an eye on him. He hadn't tried any of Kel's techniques, but she suspected that it was only a matter of time before he did, especially with as difficult as it would be to sell the breads.

Some days, Carth felt drawn to the herbalist shop. Most of the time, she stood outside, staring at the sign outside the door, standing off to the side and in the shadows, hiding as her father had taught her. The more she thought about it, the more it bothered her that she had no real trade. Staying with Vera, she might learn to run a kitchen and she might learn baking, but the only skill that offered her a way out was thieving, and that risked her safety more than anything. Had she taken the time to listen, and had she been willing to learn from her mother, she would have had another skill she could have leaned on.

It had been three days since she'd last visited the herbalist shop when she again found herself standing outside and in the shadows, watching a few people as they made their way in and then out of the shop. What did they buy? What powders or dried fruits or leaves did they come for? Was it for healing, as she suspected the older woman with the limping gait came to the herbalist for, or was it something else? Carth imagined that the young woman with the raven hair came to the herbalist for a love concoction. Her mother had scoffed at the idea that there were mixtures that would change emotion, but she had continued to mix powders specific to Carth and instructed her to take them each day.

As Carth waited, she pulled one of her mother's books from her pockets and flipped through the pages. She might not be able to read any of the writing, but a few of the pages had pictures, diagrams with labels written in Ih, mostly of plants or leaves or fruits. An herbalist guidebook of sorts. When Carth had discovered this, she began to wonder if the old woman would be able to help translate it for her.

The shop emptied again and she waited, uncertain if another would come to the shop. No one did, so Carth crept slowly, making her way across the street and to the door. Once there, she hesitated. Would she bother the woman by coming again?

Pushing open the door, she found the main portion of the shop empty.

Carth looked around, expecting the herbalist to come from behind the counter, but she did not. "Hello?"

Silence answered her.

Carth peeked behind the counter, but the old woman wasn't there. Hadn't she just been here?

A door led out the back of the shop and Carth considered going through it, seeing where the herbalist might have gone, but she didn't want to scare her, especially not when she had questions.

Carth returned to the main portion of the shop, determined to wait, and looked at the jars of powders. The flatwort was gone, the space where the jar had been now missing. Curious, Carth made her way to the back of the counter, looking for the jar of gardash, but didn't see it there either.

She felt a flush of embarrassment that she would even be looking. The herbalist had been kind to her and had offered help and suggestions when Kel had needed something to obscure his injury, and this was how she would repay her?

After waiting for a while longer, Carth left the shop. As soon as she did, she felt something off.

Her skin felt tight and there was a heaviness to the air, an energy of sorts, like there would be with a coming rain, only the cloudless sky didn't call out that there would be rain.

With a fluttering of her heart, she quickly crossed the street, receding into the alley. From this alley, she could wind her way back to River Road, and from there she could hide in the tavern. Carth receded into the shadowed space between the buildings. Would she even see anything? It was possible that she detected nothing more than her imagination and that the A'ras hadn't ventured this way.

A flash of color appeared on the street. Carth recognized the dark maroon of the A'ras. Three men made their way down the street. One had a sash of color wrapped around his upper arm. He was thick with muscle and his hair was cut short, revealing a few scars that gleamed in the sunlight. A wrap over his face obscured everything but his eyes. The man next to him was larger, appearing almost soft, but the eyes that searched the street were not. The third man was of average build, and a maroon wrap covered his entire face.

Carth willed herself back, wanting nothing more than to stay hidden in the shadows. That had been another game her father had played with her, though she was never as good at it as some of the others. In the shadows, he claimed that she could hide from almost anyone, if only she learned to find the edge. She'd never discovered what he meant by that. Probably another of his tricks. Her father had many tricks, most of them ways to keep her from finding him. If only he hadn't been so good at his tricks, she might have been able to find him before the A'ras, and before he disappeared.

They paused near her. "Do you sense it?" the muscular man asked. Carth noted the curved sword at his side, and her hand reached for the knife she'd stolen from the dead A'ras.

"There was power here." This came from the man with the hard eyes.

"Not *was*."

Carth was surprised by the voice. Not a man's like the others—this came from a woman.

Now the average build made more sense, as did the simple robe she wore. The wrap that covered her face would cover her hair as well. Carth didn't note any sword, but that didn't mean she would be unarmed. The A'ras always carried weapons, but even when they didn't, they had their magic, which made them dangerous.

"You think there is something still here? We would have sensed it had they entered the city."

The woman shot the hard-eyed man a withering glare. Carth shrunk back, moving as silently as she could and wishing that she could shrink into the shadows even more and find a way that they couldn't reach her through them.

The woman stopped moving. Her eyes scanned the street. "Do you not feel it?"

"I feel nothing."

"Because you have no subtlety," the woman said. "Focus. There was power used here. The Reshian were here."

Carth wished she could hide better. She wanted no part of the battle between the A'ras and the Reshian.

"Then we should find Al—"

"Shad would not reach us in time, and he must still recover. The attack nearly ended him. Had he not been so careful, it *would* have ended him."

She made a motion and the other two A'ras spread out on either side of her, searching the street. Carth didn't move. She wouldn't let herself move. Doing so would only risk drawing attention to her, risking revealing her position. So far, they hadn't noticed her, but how much longer would that remain true?

If only she could steady the pounding of her heart. It sounded loud to her, and she worried that her own fear would give her away. A bead of sweat formed on her brow and began a steady, irritating trickle down the side of her face. Carth refused to move and wipe it away, even when it dripped into her eye.

One of the A'ras—she could no longer tell which—appeared in the mouth of the alley.

She didn't dare move, but at the same time, she *wanted* to move. If she could take even a step back, slide away from the A'ras, she thought she would have a chance were she to need to run.

He took a step into the alley.

Carth knew she had been found.

She spun, and sprinted.

A'ras shouts followed her, but she had lived here long enough now that she knew the ways of hiding, and she raced through the streets, winding first toward the docks, then away. The shouts following her grew ever more distant, until she thought she had gotten away.

When she slowed, she discovered that she had run almost to the temple.

Why would she have ended up here? Was it coincidence that she'd returned to the same place she had come after her parents had disappeared, or had the A'ras somehow chased her here, guiding her?

She walked along the street, keeping her eyes alert as she scanned for other A'ras, but saw nothing that was out of place.

Sighing heavily, she allowed herself to relax. She had escaped the A'ras again, but how many more times did she really think she'd be able to do it? Eventually she would get herself caught if she kept doing the same thing. Better to remain hidden near the docks and not draw attention to herself.

Yet, wasn't that what she wanted? Didn't she *want* a way to get revenge for her parents and attack the A'ras?

Carth turned away from the temple.

She slowly made her way back toward the docks, but watched the street as she went, searching for signs of the A'ras. They would still be out there. Maybe not after her, but she had drawn their attention in spite of not wanting to do so.

Night had fallen by the time she made it back to River Road. There were the steady and now-familiar sounds from the docks of vendors shouting to passersby, selling meats and breads and spices. How did Vera really expect them to compete with that? They were too young to sell effectively. Most who might be interested saw their age and thought to take advantage.

Other noises filled the air here as well. Mixed with the loud cries of the vendors were the steady murmuring of dozens of voices. They were loud during the day but grew even louder when night fell, mixing with music coming from taverns like the Wounded Lyre and the steady washing of water over the rocks. All of it mixed together to give a certain rhythm to life near the river, a pulse of sorts. It had been unsettling when she had first come here, but now she was a part of it, and the noise comforted her in some ways.

Approaching the Lyre, she noticed something felt off. Carth couldn't quite place what bothered her, but it set her heart thrumming again, much as it had when she had been chased by the A'ras.

When she reached the Wounded Lyre, she found a somber atmosphere inside. Kel sat at a table picking at food, rather than making his way through the crowd, practicing at collecting scraps. Etan was nowhere to be seen, but neither was Stiv.

Carth stopped next to Kel. "What is it?"

He barely looked up. "Go away, Carth."

She sat down and forced him to notice her. "What happened?"

Kel looked up, and she could tell he'd been crying. His jaw clenched, looking like he wanted to hide that fact. "Nothing happened. We're strays. I just forgot about that fact."

"What does that mean?"

"It means we're strays."

He turned his focus back to the hunk of bread lying on

the table in front of him, picking at it slowly. Carth could tell he wouldn't say anything more.

She stood and circled around the tavern, but there was nothing here for her. She might be able to collect some scraps, but that was all she would find—scraps. Nothing like the wealthier men she'd taken to targeting as they came off the riverboats.

For Etan to be missing wasn't all that uncommon, especially these days, but where was Stiv?

She entered the kitchen, expecting to see him there, but found only Vera. She worked at a ball of dough, pressing it flat before lifting it and flipping it again, coating it in flour as she did. She moved with a steady rhythm, one where she barely blinked when Carth appeared next to her, not disrupted at all by her presence.

"Why is Kel so upset?" she asked.

Vera glanced over. "Kel should be clearing the tables. That's what I asked him to do."

"He'll get to it," she said, not wanting to get Kel into any trouble. He always seemed to find enough on his own. "But what happened? Why does he seem so upset?"

Vera pressed on the dough and flipped it over again. "I told him not to get too attached. Never does any good."

"Attached to what?"

"That boy," Vera said.

"Stiv?" Carth asked. "What happened to him?"

Vera stopped kneading the dough and met Carth's eyes. "We do all we can to protect you. That's why you're here. But there are limits, girl, that even we can't avoid."

Vera returned to kneading the dough. Carth waited for her to say something more, but she didn't. When it became clear that she would not, Carth made her way past Vera and out of the kitchen, hurrying down the hall to their room.

Inside, she found Etan sitting on his bunk with a new hole in the wall near his head. He barely glanced up when she entered.

"Where is he?" she said to him.

"Don't pretend that you care," Etan said.

"I care. What happened to him?"

"The same thing that will happen to all of us. We're strays. We're here until they get tired of us. Don't think you're so special that it won't happen to you, too."

Carth crouched down to his level. A flutter rolled through her chest as she did, never certain that Etan wouldn't snap and hit her, but she needed to know. "Did Vera and Hal do something?"

He snorted. "No. They didn't do anything."

"Then what happened?"

"You want to know? That's the problem with us being down here. Nothing happens. No one cares what happens to us. They might give us a place to sleep and offer us the scraps and leftovers from the tavern, but do they really care?"

"Vera and Hal keep us safe."

"Do they? If they kept us safe, then that kid would still be here instead of caught by *them*. Your day will come, too, Carth. Don't think you're protected. Best if you find real protection. That's what I plan on."

"What are you *talking* about?"

He snorted again. "It don't matter. It never did. We're just biding our time, aren't we? Collecting scraps until the next."

"What next?"

Etan sat up quickly and shook his head. "Like I said. It don't matter. Best find a way to keep yourself safe. Especially don't matter when you're caught. They won't say nothing then, not for you, not for me, and not for the kid."

Carth thought she understood now.

Stiv had been caught collecting scraps. The penalty for stealing was steep, and though she knew it, she'd taken to treating it as something of a game when it should not have been. Had Stiv been caught because of her?

Carth refused to let herself believe that. She hadn't taught Stiv to collect scraps. If anything, it would have been Etan and Kel who were responsible.

Watching Etan, she realized that he felt the same way.

He stood and pushed past her, leaving the room.

Carth looked around, feeling confused, wishing that either Etan or Kel or even Vera would tell her what was going on, and where Stiv had gone.

Chapter 14

In the days that followed, answers didn't come. Anytime she tried bringing up the question of what happened to Stiv, Kel became somber and withdrawn. She'd tried asking Vera again, but she'd refused to answer. Even Hal had fallen silent.

Carth rarely saw Etan any more. Usually by morning, he was up and gone before she and Kel were awake and often didn't return until well after dark. She didn't know if he continued collecting scraps, but he didn't appear hungry or poorly dressed. A shadow of scruff grew on his face now, making him look both older and rougher. The times she did see him, he had a hard, almost angry gleam in his eye.

She became worried about what would happen to her. If Stiv had been caught, how long would it really be before the rest of them were, too? Etan preferred to crash into people as he lifted their purses, and Kel wasn't much different. When one—or both—of them were caught, what would she do?

There was nothing that she *could* do.

Was that what she wanted? Did she *want* to become a thief, always worried about the next thing that would happen to her? She didn't have any other options, did she?

She found herself standing in front of the herbalist shop once more. The last time she'd come, the A'ras had been here, the same night Stiv had been caught and taken away. The A'ras continued to patrol through here, but not with regularity, and she'd managed to sneak off whenever she saw any sign of them making their way toward the docks. Still, there was more of an A'ras presence than there ever had been before.

As she watched, no one entered the herbalist, not as they had the last time.

Carth pushed through her fear and entered the shop.

It had been nearly destroyed.

Carth's stomach dropped.

The air no longer carried the scent of the leaves and oils. Bins were toppled, with dried fruits piled onto the floor. Jars of leaves had been thrown to the ground, leaving the jars cracked and destroyed. Even the oils had been spilled, streaks of wetness running down the walls and pooling on the floorboards.

She stepped around the herbs and made her way behind the counter, expecting more of the same. Boxes there were tipped over, some appearing to have been slammed to the ground, leaving the contents spilled. Two splintered chairs left a trail of debris toward the back door.

Carth paused at the counter, leaning on it and breathing heavily. This wasn't new damage. Whatever had happened here had been at least a day or two ago; otherwise, the air would smell more pungently of leaves and oil.

Nothing really remained. What appeared to be boot marks trampled over the leaves. Tiny shards of glass mixed with them. Even the dried fruits and berries had been stomped.

She shouldn't be here.

The thought came overwhelmingly to her, filling her with a sort of dread. Shops weren't just destroyed like this, were they? And it couldn't be a coincidence that the A'ras had come through here and now the shop was destroyed.

Pausing at the window, she peered out, looking into the street, fearful that someone might be watching for her, but she saw no movement. Maybe it would be better to go out through the back door anyway.

As she passed through the shop, she paused at the counter again. A flash of glass caught her eye. At first, she thought it was another broken jar and stepped carefully, remembering what the herbalist had told her about the shadesbreath, but found an intact jar.

She lifted it and realized this *was* the jar of shadesbreath.

If the herbalist was right, shadesbreath would be dangerous. She needed to be careful with it, but then, she shouldn't leave it here either, should she? Not if someone else might come along and not know what it was. Better that she remove it and store or dispose of it so that no one got hurt.

Carth slipped it into her pocket, making sure to put in the other pocket, the one without the A'ras knife.

At the back door to the shop, she paused before pushing the door open a crack and peering out. The shop opened into an empty alley and she hurried outside, closing the door behind her.

She started back toward the docks, but what was there for her there, other than an angry Kel, and Etan, who had grown increasingly quiet with her?

Instead, she made her way into the city.

Troubled thoughts plagued her. They were thoughts she never would have considered when her parents had been alive, but she wondered about her father, and why he was as skilled at sneaking around as he was. The worst part of that realization was knowing that she would never get the opportunity to ask him about his past, that she'd be left with the questions she now possessed.

Then her mother... her mother was an herbalist of sorts, but she had only worked with her family, not selling her concoctions like other herbalists did. How much had her mother known about her father? Was that the reason they had come to Nyaesh?

Her parents had never really told her why they traveled from city to city. They would spend months at a time in some, though they had been in Balis for nearly a year before moving to Nyaesh. When they'd moved, they had brought the packs they possessed, and not much else, and Carth had never questioned why.

Now that they were gone, she did. What would have brought her parents to this city, a place so dangerous that they refused to let Carth out of their sight? The only time she'd ever *really* been alone in Nyaesh had been after they'd died.

She reached the end of the alley and paused on Doland Street, considering whether she wanted to return to the docks. The sounds of the docks, those of gulls cawing and vendors shouting, drifted to her. The other direction led away from the docks, and toward the palace of the royal family. A familiar blue cloak caught her attention. Was that Jhon?

She started up the street and after him, keeping enough space between them that she didn't think it would look like she followed him. As she approached, she saw that it *was* Jhon, and he wasn't alone.

Carth shuffled to the side of the street, watching him, and noticed that he seemed to lean forward, speaking to a shorter someone who she couldn't clearly see. A part of her wanted to run up to him and find what he knew about her parents. He had known that her parents came from Ih-lash, which meant he might know more about her parents than she did.

Moving carefully forward, she tried watching for his cloak but lost sight of it amidst the rest of the crowd. Cursing herself for her caution, she tried finding him, but failed. Jhon had disappeared.

Carth spent the rest of the afternoon looking for him. She had questions she needed answered. Almost getting attacked by the A'ras wasn't going to change the fact that she wanted to know what more he knew about her family—and why.

Carth stood along the shore and stared out over the river. Standing here, with the sound of the gulls calling overhead and the soft rushing of water over the rocks, she would almost call it peaceful. Vera and Hal had offered her protection—though it was protection that she now understood they had paid the A'ras to provide—but the tavern was not her home. Having Jhon speak to her about her parents, and bring the questions that she had back to her mind, had made it all too clear that she didn't belong down here near the docks. There might be safety, but it was a false safety, and one that faded at the first sign of attack.

What else could she do?

She wanted to know more about Felyn. She needed to know how a man like that existed, and how he had managed to attack the A'ras as easily as he had. But the memory of Felyn terrified her.

If she could find Jhon again, she might be able to ask him the questions that bothered her, but what if she couldn't?

So far, he had found her in the tavern and near the docks. From what he had said to her, it seemed he had been shadowing her, following her once he realized who she was. That meant that he might continue to follow her.

Leaving the River Road, she started into the city, following alleys that led generally deeper into the city. As she went, she kept her eyes open for any sign that she might be followed, once more playing the game that her parents had played with her, trying to determine if someone else trailed her and searching for evidence that she wasn't alone. Her father had been quite skilled at keeping hidden, but so had her mother, both of them wanting Carth to develop the same skills.

She remembered a game where she tried to keep her father from following her, and when she discovered that he did tail her, she'd try to shake him. She had never managed to succeed, almost as if he had some otherworldly ability he hid from her.

Passing shops, she glanced in windows, using the reflection to check behind her. She took quick turns, thinking that if anyone trailed her, they would reveal themselves. Carth even took to staring up at the roofline, wondering if someone other than her father would be able to follow her from there. She found nothing.

This street led to a star-shaped intersection where two other streets met, a place within the city known as Chalice Corner. The intersection was a dangerous one for anyone with horse and carriage, but on foot, it proved easy enough to navigate. Carth paused near a streetlight, making it appear that she simply waited when really she used it as an opportunity to look all around her.

She found nothing that seemed out of place.

Had she been mistaken? Jhon had to have been following her for him to know as much about her as he did, unless he had some other way of finding out her secrets. But what would that be? There were stories of people far across the sea who could read each other's thoughts, but Carth thought that only rumor. Such things were no more possible than a person flying. No, there had to be some other explanation.

Had her parents worked with Jhon? It seemed unlikely, but then, Carth had never questioned why her parents moved cities.

Carth frowned. How could she really know so little about her own parents? And why did it seem that Jhon knew more about her family than she did in some ways?

The people moving along Chalice Road began to part, drawing her attention along the street. Chalice Road had some of the more expensive shops in Nyaesh, dressmakers and candle makers and bakers and carpet weavers and countless others that she would never have the money to afford visiting. The thought of stopping in one of the shops along Chalice Road left her feeling flushed.

Coming toward her were five A'ras.

That explained why the crowd parted.

Carth considered hiding. Standing out in the open when the A'ras came through would put her in danger, especially if she had somehow managed to draw their attention, but she didn't want to hide. She wanted to see them, and wanted to know what they might do. They served the royal family, but they also served their own purposes. That they were willing to leave the docks alone when bribed told her that they were not nearly as holy as she had been led to believe, though the brutal way they punished others didn't fit with their holy appearance, either.

The A'ras paused at the intersection. Standing alongside the lamppost, she tried to shrink against the metal, slimming herself as much as possible. She wanted to watch to see what they would do.

The A'ras paused at the corner. One of them caught her eye and looked her up and down before turning away from her, completely dismissing her.

Carth sighed as they passed. She didn't want any more attention from them anyway, but for her to be so quickly dismissed... Hal and Vera had warned her that once the A'ras identified her, she would be in danger. Here she had allowed herself to be seen, allowed them to notice her, but they hadn't shown any real interest.

Maybe it wasn't her they cared about at all.

As the A'ras moved along the street, still following Chalice Road, she decided to follow. Doing so would be dangerous and she knew better than to attempt it, but a sudden urge compelled her to do so.

Others all tried to keep out of the way of the A'ras. She used that as a distraction, letting herself drift from one area of congestion to the next, always staying just out of sight, yet close enough that she could tell where the A'ras were. Trailing them wasn't difficult; all she had to do was stay behind the spreading bubble cleared of people as they moved along the street. This time, she played the role her father had usually played, and she was the one who followed behind.

She hadn't learned his tricks for doing so as well as he did, but she knew the ways that she had used to detect him, and thought that she could mask herself so that they wouldn't pick her out quite so easily.

Quick movements were dangerous, but if she could time them to when the others around her moved more quickly, she wouldn't have to fear anything. Other than that, the challenge

SHADOW BLESSED

she had would be that she moved against the flow of traffic. That alone would cause her to stand out. To combat that, she moved in a zigzagging way, hoping that it would appear as if she followed the flow of others around her.

What was she doing, anyway? Why did she risk herself following the A'ras? She couldn't hope to learn anything other than that they were deadly and dangerous, but she already knew that. The only thing that she would discover was that she could suffer with them.

Two of the A'ras branched off, leaving the other three moving on their own. Carth debated which way to follow. If she trailed the group of the three who appeared to head toward the royal palace, she might get to see where they trained. But if she followed the pair of A'ras, she might discover what else they did in the city.

Carth followed the three.

People continued to give them space as they moved through the city, but Carth was surprised that the farther she went into the city, the less concerned people were about passing them. Whereas near the docks, people hid, the streets completely clearing, the closer she got to the palace, the less space formed around them. They still moved unencumbered, but it wasn't anything that made it seem like people were actually worried about them.

Carth followed more easily now, no longer having to seem as if she moved away from them. Now she could flow with the pace of people on the street, moving along the street behind them, tailing them closely enough that she didn't really fear being caught.

The palace gleamed in the distance. Carth had never been this close to it before. Many in the city made a point of visiting, if only to lay eyes on the royal family's home, but since living along the docks with Vera and Hal, she hadn't had the need or desire to come this deep into the city. The exposure to the man who had nearly killed Kel had been enough for her.

The A'ras passed through the gate. Carth waited, staring after them, wishing she could follow them through, but the gate led into the palace grounds. Entering through it in the daylight risked more exposure than she was willing.

She trekked on, making her way slowly along the wall before stopping. There was nothing she could do that wouldn't draw too much attention.

As she looked up at the wall, curiosity about what happened on the other side nearly overwhelmed her. She might not be able to climb it in the daylight, fearing that not only would the A'ras see her, but others along the street would and might alert the A'ras. If she waited until it was dark… then she might be able to venture over and discover what the A'ras did, and maybe how they managed some of their magic. Maybe she'd find a way to learn *why* her parents were gone. Either way, it was time to stop waiting around and get on with what needed to get done.

Chapter 15

Night fell quickly when the sun finally descended. In some parts of the city, night came on as a gradual change, a descent from the light of day to the steadily rising moon. Near the palace, it felt more abrupt. Carth decided that was good, as she didn't think that she could wait much longer.

She should have returned to the Lyre. Remaining here instead of going back to the docks would only leave Vera and Hal worried, but Carth feared that if she did go, she wouldn't have the strength of will to return. At least by remaining, she forced herself to focus on the A'ras. If she went back to the docks and to the Wounded Lyre, she wouldn't come back tonight. It was possible she wouldn't come back at all.

The longer she remained near the tall wall separating the rest of Nyaesh from the royal family, the more she thought about the A'ras. While waiting, she struggled to remember all that she could about them, trying to remember what it was her parents had taught her.

The A'ras were users of a kind of magic they were born

to, something of a blood magic. Her father had told her that once, though Carth didn't really know what that meant. There were other types of magic, some that she doubted that she'd ever experience, from people who could use different metals to create power to those with enhanced vision. Even men and women who could glimpse the future. Most power came from a combination. A person had to be born with a certain potential, and if they were, they had to find the right trigger for their power.

Carth worried that her presence here would draw attention. The longer she remained, the more she wondered if others on the street would notice her and comment about her presence, but so far she didn't think anyone had. She didn't stay in one place for too long, but didn't make any attempt to collect scraps while she was here either, not wanting to run the risk of drawing any more attention to herself than needed. Every so often, she squeezed the hilt of the knife she carried, using it as a reassurance that she would be fine.

As the sun set and the moon began to rise, a strange drumming began to build.

Carth listened, wondering if it came from the other side of the wall, but then realized that it came from within the city. Other instruments joined the drumming, lifting into the night with a celebratory energy that had her foot tapping before she realized what she did. Her body felt pulled by the music, drawn away from the wall.

She followed the sound, a mixture of curiosity and the knowledge that she had time to spare pulling her along the street. It came not from a tavern, but from a small square where a crowd of people danced along to the music. The sounds built, stronger and stronger, a steady drumming that mixed with piercing horns and the sweet sounds of the lyre. A fire leaped toward the sky, giving a bright light to the night.

What festival was this?

Men wore costumes, masks over their faces, and most had long robes as well. Women were dressed more scantily. More than a few barely covered their breasts, and had chosen tight wraps that left little to the imagination, revealing their curves. Carth's plain dress was out of place here.

Street vendors had set up shop. Some sold roasted meats and breads, and others had mugs of ale available. The festivities drew her in and she longed to be a part of them, but that wasn't the reason she was here.

Carth pulled herself away from the festival, hoping she would have time to return before the night was over, but she intended to climb the wall. With the revelry, there was already a distraction, one that she could use to her advantage.

When she reached the wall, darkness had set in fully, and she quickly scaled the wall, not wanting to linger any longer.

She didn't let herself think about what she did. If she considered the climb, and the fact that it would take nothing more than a few people noticing her to draw the attention of the A'ras, she would have gone running back to the docks. A desire for answers—or if not answers, at least knowledge— pulled her over.

On the other side, she clung to the stone, searching for

shadows, but there were none. Ivy crept along the stone and copses of trees grew in places, mixed with rows of hedges lining walkways. Lanterns fought against the darkness, each blazing with a bright yellow light that pushed back the night. She ducked behind the hedges, using them as a barrier to keep from getting noticed as she slipped through the palace grounds.

With each step, she couldn't shake the feeling that she shouldn't be here. If the royal family discovered her, she would be dragged off to prison, or possibly a much worse fate, one where they would torment her. Then the prospect of losing a hand for collecting scraps wouldn't seem quite so bad.

Yet, if she could understand the A'ras, then she could chase down information about Felyn and eventually learn what had happened to her parents. That was all that she cared about anymore.

Carth moved carefully along the grounds, but no one else was out. The walkways were empty and she saw nothing, not even any sign of guards. She might as well follow the paths openly rather than hide as she did.

She trailed along the hedge. The music from the festival pressed against her, a pulsing sort of rhythm that became more muted the farther she slunk away from the wall, but she still could hear elements of the music, like the occasional loud shriek from one of the horns, or a heavier drumming as the music reached a crescendo. It gave a sense of urgency to the night.

The lantern light faded as she neared the palace, the space

between the lanterns spreading, casting greater shadows that stretched longer. Carth lingered in the shadows, using them to obscure herself, thinking of how her father had taught her to use the darkness to her advantage. That had been another game, but one she had only been in the early stages of learning.

A flicker of movement caught her attention.

Carth hesitated, wishing she could drape herself in darkness, wanting to pull it around her like a blanket to hide within. She refused to move, not daring to risk exposing herself here. There came another movement, but she couldn't see what it was.

Her heart hammered heavily—and probably loudly. If she didn't move, she would be caught. She was too in the open, too exposed, but moving—even a little—would draw more attention.

Letting out a slow breath, she thought of what her father had taught her of sinking into the shadows. *Let it surround you. Shadow is as real as light, only shadow you can use.*

His voice drifted to the forefront of her mind, making her miss him more than she had in some time. She could almost hear his words the same as she had heard them when he'd whispered them in her ear when she had first learned.

Sink into the shadows. Draw them around you like a cloak.

Movement appeared closer. Carth considered making a run for it, but that would definitely draw attention. What she needed was a way to do what her father had instructed.

Think like the shadow and become a part of it.

A flush washed through her and her skin felt warm. A

cold sweat beaded on her brow and she barely considered wiping it away.

Find the edge of darkness and use it.

Carth's gaze darted around the grounds. A muted voice came to her, as if through a fog. Near one of the lanterns, she found an edge of darkness, but how to use it?

She stared at it, focusing on it, wishing to be a part of it so that she could hide.

Night thickened around her.

Carth didn't move.

Footsteps tapped along cobbles, but the sound seemed to come from a distance, different than what it should have been. The voice came again, at once more distant and closer, a strange combination. She stood unmoving, a statue in the night, praying that shadows would remain around her and keep her hidden.

Slowly, the sound and the movement eased.

This had been the stupidest thing she had ever done. Why risk coming here? What did she really think she could learn? The A'ras might find her, and if they did, she would be dead before she could get any answers.

With her heart still hammering, she turned and slowly, steadily, made her way back toward the wall. She stayed hidden between the shadows of the lanterns. Thankfully, they seemed dimmer than before, more willing to hide her. As she climbed up the wall, she paused near the top, the crawling sensation along her spine making her think someone had noticed her. Without waiting any longer, she dropped to the other side and hurried into the crowd, praying that she hadn't been seen.

As the throng of people out celebrating surrounded her, she saw a shimmering cloak and a flash of maroon behind her, and realized that she must have been.

Chapter 16

Carth hurried forward. As much as she might want to run, she knew that running would only draw even more attention. At least by going in a controlled fashion, walking at a fast but reasonable pace, she could blend into the crowd. She made her way toward the music, wanting to let the rhythmic sounds of the festival help hide her and knowing that the busier that it was, the easier time she would have of hiding.

A shout from behind her told her that the A'ras neared.

Carth moved more quickly. She bounced off a few people and slipped around others. There would be no hiding in shadows here, nothing of the darkness that she could use to protect herself. Finding her way to safety meant getting free of the A'ras tailing her, if she could.

She thought of how she had always managed to follow her mother. Carth had used the sounds of her footsteps and the color of her hair or her dress to keep a visual connection. With the sound of the festival, she didn't have to worry about noise, but her dress stood out. What she needed was a costume.

And quickly.

She bumped into another man, this one with a well-cut robe, his face shielded by a mask made of black lace that surrounded his eyes. Carth dipped her hand into his pocket as she bumped into him, pulling out his coin purse before hurrying away.

At least now she had a way to pay for a costume.

She hurried to the side of the street, searching for the vendors. They were less frequent here, though as she made her way toward the music, the crowd thickened, making it more difficult to move quickly. The A'ras would have no such challenges. People moved out of their way, not wanting to suffer their wrath or risk their sword. What Carth wouldn't give to have that kind of power.

There! She saw a vendor selling masks… and gowns.

She tipped the contents of the purse into her hand and counted. Five silver vens. Would that be enough?

It seemed a fortune, especially considering how excited Kel and Etan got when they managed to find a couple coppers, but this was near the palace and there would be a difference in price.

She hurried to the stand, risking a glance over her shoulder.

Not only one A'ras, but two. And they headed toward her.

"How much for the mask?" Carth asked the vendor quickly.

The man had a bulbous bright red nose, and as he leaned toward her, a leering grin crossed his face. "Girl like you out for the Laseer Festival alone?"

She shook her head, thinking quickly. The fact that he commented on her age made her suddenly aware that she was the youngest person around. There had been no children at this festival.

What had she been thinking?

There would be time for berating herself later. For now, she needed to hide.

"Girl? I'm nearly eighteen," Carth said, pulling her back straighter and thrusting out her chest slightly. There was no way that she could pass for eighteen normally, but maybe with the festival and with people drunk on ale and wine, she might have a chance. "And my future husband is..." She made a show of looking around, noting that the A'ras were within two dozen steps of her. The crowd was thicker here, slowing them, but there was little doubt that they came in her direction. "Over there." She pointed to a muscular man near her. "How much for the mask?"

The vendor's gaze drifted to the man and then back to Carth. "Four vens."

Carth gritted her teeth. Four. The money was not hers and she didn't really have the time to bargain with him anyway, but the price was outrageous. "Throw in the gown and I'll give you five." She set the stack of silver on the counter in front of him.

The man started to look past her. If he saw the A'ras, he would be less likely to finish the transaction.

"What do you say? Or should I have my future husband come make a bargain?" she asked sweetly.

The vendor's gaze pulled back down to her and he

smiled, grabbing a rolled gown and one of his masks and handing them to her.

Carth took them and spun, hurrying to the side.

She ducked down, slipping on the mask and quickly unrolling the robe, hoping that it fit well enough. It didn't have to be perfect. Few that she'd seen wore anything too well fitted, but she didn't want to give the A'ras any reason to notice her.

The crowd began to part behind her.

That was all the sign that she needed to know that the A'ras were near.

She stood carefully and made a show of standing close to a man near her. She wasn't tall enough for eighteen and had to stand on her toes to look taller, but at least this way she could create the impression of being with someone.

As the crowd separated around the A'ras, she followed the man. He had a muscular build and his robe draped to the ground, dragging behind him, so that Carth had to be careful she didn't step on it. He glanced at her, and she smiled, hoping that he wouldn't try anything.

The A'ras moved past.

Carth tensed, her hand reaching for her pocket and the knife she carried with her. If nothing else, she could attack them and use the chaos of the festival to hide.

What had gotten into her? Could she really be thinking about attacking the A'ras this openly? Attacking would be suicide.

Unless she could sneak behind them.

They were responsible for what had happened to her

mother. She might not have seen how they killed her, but the A'ras had been there. She might not get vengeance on Felyn—Carth didn't want to see him again—but there was the hope that she could find a way to get some revenge on the A'ras.

She left the man, slipping away from him as she wound through the crowd, slipping behind the A'ras. She followed them, letting the way the crowd parted ahead of her guide her. As she went, she pulled the knife from within her pocket.

The knife felt cold in her hand, colder than it had ever felt before.

Maybe that was because the knife knew what she intended.

As she approached the A'ras, barely only five paces away, they turned toward her.

Had she made a mistake? Had they known that she was there?

Carth didn't think that she'd been that loud. She glanced around and realized that no one else approached the A'ras. She stood alone in the middle of a crowd, wearing a mask and a gown and holding a knife.

One of the A'ras glanced at the knife.

They reached for their swords as one.

Carth froze. She wanted to run, to disappear and find a place where they wouldn't reach her, but the crowd grew more and more distant as she stood there, as if they withdrew, knowing what the A'ras would do.

There was no way she would be able to use this knife

against them, not when they came at her with swords.

The knife went colder in her hand.

Her skin burned with energy and felt as if it were pulled tight, as if she'd been standing in the sun for too long. A strange muffling filled her ears and she became unaware of anything else, unable to take her eyes off the A'ras.

They approached her casually. There was no urgency, no concern that she might run or that she might attack them. These were men who knew that she would—that she could—go nowhere.

Was this the effect of their magic?

There were stories of the A'ras magic, but she'd never experienced it before. She had never wanted to.

Carth tried pulling away. If nothing else, she could slip the knife back into her pocket, try to pretend that she hadn't carried it, or that she hadn't intended to use it against the A'ras. Her hand wouldn't work. Nothing worked, as if her mind couldn't control her body.

The knife remained cold, practically burning her skin.

The A'ras were almost upon her.

She could smell them now, a mixture of scents that reminded her of the herbalist shop. Notes of pine and slick oil combined together, the effect intoxicating. One of the swords moved, and Carth followed its movement.

"Kneel."

The voice was gravelly and she could do nothing but obey.

She went to her knees, staring at the A'ras and the wrap around his head that covered his mouth and chin, leaving only his eyes visible. A part of her mind rebelled, raging to stand, to fight, to do anything but what the A'ras wanted of her, but she didn't. She couldn't.

As much as she wanted to slip the knife away and hide it, her hand wouldn't move.

The only thing that seemed to work was her mind. It raced, running through the terrifying thoughts of what would happen to her. Would the A'ras simply end her here, or would they try ask her why she had climbed the wall into the palace yard? What would she answer if they did?

"What is your name?" the other A'ras said. He didn't have the same wrap around his head, but the thick beard on his chin hid his lips as he spoke.

"Carth." She answered in spite of her desire *not* to answer, in spite of the fact that she knew that she should not answer. Giving her name to the A'ras meant that were she able to escape, they would have a way to find her.

"Where did you obtain that blade?" the bearded man asked.

"The A'ras."

The man stepped closer. Strangely, he appeared to hesitate. "You would not have taken a knife from one of the A'ras."

"They were dead."

The bearded man glanced at the other. "They?"

"There were three. They were killed."

"She lies, Ah-rahn."

The bearded man stared at the knife. "Does she? Look at the blade she carries. Remember what happened to Al-shad."

Carth had heard that name before, but didn't know when. Where had she heard it?

"Give me the knife."

She wanted nothing more than to hand the knife to the A'ras, but her arm didn't work. She couldn't lift it and couldn't release the hilt of the blade.

"The knife," Ah-rahn said. "Hand it to me."

Carth tried, but it was as if the chill in the blade prevented her from lifting her hand. She could no more hand the knife to him than she could open her mouth and refuse.

The other A'ras took a step toward her. Carth readied for the swing of his sword and the inevitable pain, but then there would be nothing, and she would be reunited with her mother and father. Would that not be worth the brief pain?

The A'ras with the wrap over his face grunted and fell to the ground.

Carth wanted to look to see what had happened, but Ah-rahn approached, his sword already moving. She couldn't even close her eyes; she would have to watch as the sword struck.

Ah-rahn took another step toward her. It seemed as if time slowed. His sword swung.

And then stopped.

His head tipped to the side and a confused expression crossed his face. His sword dropped from his hand and clattered to the stone. As it did, whatever spell held her in place released her.

Carth jumped to her feet and jabbed the knife at him,

wanting to stab him in the stomach or chest, wanting revenge for her parents, but someone grabbed her wrist.

She jerked her hand away, trembling with fear. When she turned, she expected another A'ras, but there was not.

Instead, a familiar face looked at her. Rather than a blank and unreadable expression as he usually wore, concern pulled at the corners of Jhon's eyes. "Easy," he said softly.

"What are you doing here?"

He glanced over her shoulder. "I would ask you the same, but it seems that we don't have time for questions. Perhaps we can speak if we get free of this."

Jhon pulled on her arm, dragging her down the street, away from the palace. Carth hazarded a look over her shoulder and noted that three more A'ras appeared. One stopped and knelt next to the two that had attacked her, while the other two continued after them. Her skin felt tight and she detected the strange sizzling sensation on her flesh that she'd noticed when the A'ras used their magic before.

"You will have to obscure us," Jhon said.

"I don't know what you mean."

"Like you did in the palace yard. If we are to escape, you will have to obscure us. Now that they have sighted me, that is the only way we'll get free of them."

The corners of his eyes twitched, the same way her father's did when he struggled. She glanced back and realized that the A'ras still trailed her, and wondered if they had used their magic to attack.

"Hurry!" Jhon urged. He pulled them into an alley. The tight sensation to her skin didn't change.

"I don't know what you mean. How can I obscure us?"

Jhon pushed her up against the wall, flattening them into the growing darkness. "You are shadow blessed, Carth of Ihlash."

"Shadow blessed?"

"There's no time to explain now. You must repeat what you did on the palace grounds. I followed you, but then you disappeared. There is only one way you would disappear from me, the same way you managed to hide me when your friend attacked. I should have seen it earlier."

The only thing she had done was try to sink into the shadows. That had been the trick her father had demonstrated, a way of masking herself. It was one she'd struggled with, and now he claimed it made her shadow blessed?

"They are almost upon us," Jhon said more calmly than she felt.

Her heart raced, panic setting in. She didn't need for Jhon to tell her that the A'ras were nearly upon them. She could feel the dangerous pull of their magic, the way her skin felt and the sizzling energy that crackled in the air.

What she had done in the palace yard had been attempting to sink into the shadows. Could she really do that? Was there some sort of magic to her?

Her skin sizzled even more, growing ever tighter.

Carth couldn't delay attempting.

She focused on the shadows around them, searching for the edge of it as her father had taught her, and found it near the mouth of the alley. Once she found it, she pulled on it, drawing the shadows around her as she did, letting herself fade backward into the darkness, into the shadows.

Darkness grew like a fog around her. Jhon became almost insubstantial next to her. Sounds became muted. She held her breath, afraid to do anything, afraid to say anything.

The tension faded from her skin, and the energy in the air dissipated somewhat.

Muted footsteps thudded past. Through the darkness, Carth caught sight of a hint of maroon and recognized the A'ras passing.

The footsteps paused.

Carth's heart thudded in her chest. Jhon did not move, though she wondered if she would see it if he did. Would the A'ras hear her heart beating? Would they know she was here?

Then the footsteps started away, continuing down the street.

Jhon tapped her on the arm. "You may release it."

Carth didn't know how to release it, but she allowed herself to breathe and took a step forward. As she did, the darkness settled back into place, the fog lifting.

This time, there was a clear sense that she had done something, though she wasn't exactly certain what it was. "How is that possible?" she asked.

"You are shadow blessed," Jhon said again. "Come with me, and I will explain as much as is safe."

Chapter 17

Carth stood atop a stooped roof, looking down at the city. Was this the sort of view her father had had when he had crawled along the roofs? From here, she just made out the edge of the river, a black line where the lights of the city ended.

"Why did you risk going to the palace garden tonight?" Jhon asked. He stood on the edge of the roof, his hands clasped behind him as he studied the night.

Carth kept back from the edge. She wasn't afraid of heights so much as she was terrified of them. She debated how much to answer Jhon, but then without him, she wouldn't have been able to get away from the A'ras. "You killed two of them," she said.

He made an expression like he'd just eaten rotten fish. "Not killed, but I fear they will not see it any differently. Besides, it could not have been helped, not if you were to get free. Had you not approached as you did, it might not have been necessary."

Carth flushed. Anger had overcome her when she had

finally managed to get free of the A'ras magic.

"An interesting knife you have."

She reached into her pocket and squeezed the hilt. Did he know that it was one of the A'ras knives?

"Few are able to safely possess such a blade."

"It's an A'ras blade."

He arched a brow. "Is it? Those who hold one of the A'ras blades usually suffer in some ways."

"What do you mean, they suffer?"

"You felt the power the A'ras are able to work. They place some of that power into their swords and knives. It is why they are so dangerous."

"I thought they were poisoned."

"Perhaps some. Others use their particular brand of magic through the blade."

Carth relaxed her grip on the knife. Was it the same way?

"Weapons are crafted by the A'ras, and typically linked in some ways to the maker. That gives them greater strength, and makes them more dangerous as well."

"A man named Al-shad had this one."

A half-smile tugged at his lips, almost amused. "Did he give it to you?"

Carth shook her head. "He... he was one of the A'ras who..." She swallowed and couldn't finish.

"Your mother?"

She nodded.

"You were there that day."

She nodded again, her hand slipping into her pocket and fingering her mother's ring.

"Ah, child, you should not have been exposed to that. These are dangerous people, and that"—he pointed to her pocket where she held the knife, the hilt no longer biting cold as it had been—"was made by a man with much power."

He touched her head and a warmth washed through her. It happened briefly, so quickly that she couldn't react.

"Why did you help me? Why have you been following me, for that matter?"

Jhon looked at her for a moment, then turned back to stare out over the city. "What do you know of your place of birth?" he asked.

"I don't know anything. My parents rarely spoke of Ih-lash."

"Yet they taught you many of the lessons of the people."

"Like what?"

"There are skills that are—or were—taught to the children of Ih-lash. They would learn to follow without being seen. They would learn to see what wished to remain hidden. They would be able to slip in without others knowing, and disappear again." Jhon looked over his shoulder at her. "I can see from your expression that you have some familiarity with what I am telling you."

"The games," she said. When he frowned, she went on. "My parents used to play games like that with me. I would trail my mother, but as it went on, I had to remain a certain distance from her. Eventually, I had to let her get so far ahead that I couldn't see her. That was what we were doing that day… that day…"

183

She swallowed the lump in her throat, trying to keep from crying again. Every time she thought of that day, tears welled in her eyes unbidden. She hadn't managed to find a way to keep them from coming.

"That is why you weren't with them when they were discovered," Jhon said.

She nodded. "My father was behind me. Watching me. My mother…"

The image of her mother lying on the street, unmoving, came into her mind. It was an image that came to her while she slept, and often while she was awake. The complete lack of concern from Felyn or the A'ras made it even more difficult for her to bear.

"Were there other games your parents played with you?" he asked.

Carth nodded. "There were many."

"Tell me about them."

Carth didn't *want* to share those stories with a stranger, but if she didn't, if she didn't explain what she had been through and share with him what her parents had done with her, would Jhon ever help her understand *why* they were gone? Answers were the thing she wanted most of all, and here she was with a man who seemingly had them.

So she shared with Jhon the details of the games she had played with her parents. As she did, Jhon watched her, his face unreadable. When she got to describing how she sank into the shadows, he actually smiled again. As he did, the blank slate expression that he wore changed, making him appear much more youthful. In that moment, Carth wondered exactly how old he actually was. In some ways, he didn't appear that much older than her.

"That is what proves you are shadow blessed," Jhon said.

"What is shadow blessed?"

"There are few, even in Ih-lash, but the games you describe are meant to determine who is born with those gifts. Most in Ih-lash are able to move without being seen, but the shadow blessed, they are able to do something else entirely. Not only can they move without being seen, but they can manipulate the shadows, make it so that darkness shrouds them. In Ih-lash, it is considered a particularly blessed skill to possess."

"Why do you think that I am shadow blessed?"

"There are telltale signs one can look for. When I first discovered you, the way you moved made it clear that you had the skills of one of Ih-lash. That intrigued me. It had been years since I had come across someone of Ih-lash who was not a part of…" He seemed to catch himself and smiled. "No matter. Only know that it intrigued me. And still does."

Years? Carth would have guessed Jhon no older than his early twenties, but the way he spoke made it sound as if he were much older, unless he had been training for such a long time.

"I have trailed you. When you shrouded me near the river, I suspected, but with this," he tapped his head where remnants of the bruise remained, "I knew with certainty."

Carth flushed. "Kel is sorry about that."

Jhon shrugged. "I live. That is more than most who come across the A'ras in that state can claim. But for you to have hidden me, that takes a skill that few possess. I waited, watching you as you made your way into the city. Consider me curious. And then I find that you climbed over the wall, putting yourself in danger by going into the palace yard. I watched, unable to enter myself, only to see that you were not in the danger that I expected."

Too many questions came to mind for her to pick only one. "But you knew my name. You knew where I was from before then."

Jhon shrugged, the barest movement of his shoulders.

There was more than what he told her. Why wouldn't he share?

"Are you from Ih-lash?" she asked. That seemed the one that she most wanted to ask. It would explain why he had recognized her heritage when she tried to lie about it, and how he knew as much as he did about the games.

"I am not. I have studied with one who is."

"Studied?"

He nodded.

"Can he teach me?"

"He is not in Nyaesh, and I would not be able to bring you to him."

Carth turned away to hide her disappointment. All she had wanted was to understand what had happened to her parents, but now she had other questions she wanted answered. Now that she knew her parents had known her to be shadow blessed, why would they have taken her from Ih-lash? If her ability was considered blessed in their homeland, why take her from it?

"Then why do you follow me?" she asked.

Jhon smiled. "Many reasons, but curiosity might be the most apt. I have never met someone shadow blessed before. As I have said, even in Ih-lash, it is a rare ability, and one that is considered particularly fortunate. Now that I have seen it, I think there is something that you can do to help me."

"How can I help you?"

Jhon lowered himself until he was at her level, crouching so that his deep gray cloak spread around him. "I have told you that I am not of Nyaesh. I am here for a reason."

"Your assets?" Carth asked.

"Partly. But there is another reason, one that I think you could help with."

"Why would I help you?"

The edges of his mouth twitched, almost as if in a smile. "You have much anger. I saw it when you attempted to attack the A'ras."

"They killed my mother. My father."

"So you have said, but what purpose does your anger serve?"

It was the same kind of question her father would have asked. "They deserved better," Carth said, trying to keep the bitterness from her voice. Jhon wouldn't understand. She had nothing else in Nyaesh. With her parents gone, there was nothing for her here. This city was to have been a stop, a brief interlude as they continued south, but now this was all that she knew. Without her parents, she could go nowhere else. Without them, she would *be* nothing else.

"They deserved better," Jhon agreed.

Carth stared at her hand, twisting her fingers together. The painful gnawing she felt in her stomach when thinking of her parents had returned. "What do you want from me?"

"You have a gift, one that might be of assistance to me while I remain in the city, much as I think I might be of assistance to you. In exchange, I will help you find what you want to know."

Carth looked up. "How?"

"I may not be shadow blessed, but I can help you understand your ability."

What would he ask of her in exchange for teaching her about her ability? Would he demand that she steal for him like she had learned to do for Vera? Would there be something else he'd ask, something equally—or more—likely to get her in trouble, possibly even end with her dead?

"What kind of things do you think you can help me learn?"

He smiled. "There are ways to use shadows, those that I have heard discussed, that I can tell you about."

"In exchange?"

"You will shroud me when asked. And you must not talk about what I ask of you."

Carth considered refusing. If she did, she could return to the docks, to the Wounded Lyre, and help Vera and Hal as they paid the bounty to keep the strays safe. She might even be able to discover ways to use her ability on her own, not needing Jhon to guide her. Hadn't she taken the first step on her own? She could to do more, learn to use the shadows as she remembered the lessons that her father had taught her, and maybe she would be able to help Vera and Hal so that they didn't have to pay off the A'ras. With such an ability, she would be able to collect even more coin and wouldn't have to fear getting caught.

But that felt too mundane, almost as if she would waste the chance to learn more about what she could do. And doing so would be a disappointment to the memory of her parents.

"When would you start?" she asked him.

This time, Jhon did smile. "How about tonight?"

Chapter 18

In the days since Jhon had revealed her ability to her, Carth had met with him a few times, always in the evenings after she had collected enough scraps to appease Vera, and always away from River Road, far enough that Kel or Etan wouldn't find her by accident.

Carth had grown increasingly comfortable with shrouding herself in shadows. Cloaking. That was what Jhon called it, and in some ways it felt much like she placed a cloak on, but in other ways it was different. She got comfortable pulling at the edge of the shadows, rolling them toward her. There was a trick to it, memories of what her father had told her making it easier. Her father had described it as finding the edge of the shadows and pulling it to her; Jhon described it more like she drew the darkness away from the edge of the light.

"Think of a pool of darkness as it sits between two lanterns. You want to be that darkness, that place where light cannot reach. That is where the shadows will be thickest. Much like light calls to light, shadow will call to shadow."

She held those words in her mind as she pulled on the

shadows, waiting again for Jhon to return. Much of what he said reminded her of her father and the lessons he had taught. Tonight she stood in the middle of a street—one she had been to before, and one where she knew that darkness tended to linger. Pulling on the shadows was easy enough when she stood still, but harder when she attempted to move. That was what Jhon wanted her to master next. If she could move while holding on to the shadows, then she could reach anywhere. She had the sense that what he needed of her required that she would sneak him somewhere while holding on to the darkness.

Carth breathed out, forcing herself to continue to take steady breaths while holding on to the shadow. It was too easy to hold her breath, but when she did, nothing moved. For her to take this next step, she *had* to take a breath.

As the breath left her, she tried taking a step forward, pulling the shadows with her.

They slipped and she paused, trying to gather them back around her. When she stopped moving, it was much easier to focus. Jhon still hadn't told her if there was any way to be noticed while holding on to the shadows. There must be, but he wouldn't share that.

Jhon hadn't shown last night. It was the first time since he'd agreed to work with her that he hadn't appeared. Carth tried not to let that bother her, but learning that she had a talent and then trying to understand how it could be used left her feeling anxious. Besides that, she still didn't know what Jhon intended her to do, only that it had something to do with her ability.

She paused at an intersection and ducked into the shadows between a pair of streetlamps. Whereas before that had always been habit, now she did it intentionally, knowing that if she could get deeper into the shadows, she would be able to cloak herself better. She had even started to rate the different levels of darkness. Some shadows were deeper, and she found it easier to cloak herself in those places, almost as if the darkness *wanted* her to gather it.

As she practiced cloaking herself, voices drifted down the street.

Carth moved along the walls, making her way toward the sound of the voices, not attempting to use the shadows yet. Not that she would be able to do so while she moved anyway.

Was it Jhon?

When he'd rescued her from the river, there had been another with him, but she hadn't seen him with anyone else since then. And the voices made no effort to hide, speaking more loudly than she would have expected were it Jhon. He was careful, measured in the way he spoke, and she doubted he would risk himself like that.

"Stop kickin'."

Carth froze. She was too near a streetlight but pulled on the shadows anyway, drawing them around her. They shifted, unfurling from the pools of darkness between the lanterns and sliding toward her. It would look unnatural, and she knew that. That had been one of Jhon's warnings. *Use the darkness as it appears.* Cloaking as she did now appeared unusual and would draw attention to her.

"Maybe she'll stop kicking when you stop squeezing her arm so tight."

Carth couldn't quite see who spoke. They were across the street and behind buildings, but their voice carried to her, muted in that strange way things sounded when the darkness shrouded her.

"Gotta squeeze or she'll wriggle free!"

Carth had to know what was going on.

She moved away from the lantern, where the darkness should be. As she did, she felt the shadows shift with her. She almost let out a whoop of excitement. That was the first time she had managed to move *with* the shadows.

Pausing a moment, she collected herself, holding on to the shadows again before continuing toward the voices.

As she did, she couldn't maintain her connection and the shadows slipped away from her.

"Quit it now, or you'll get the hand again!"

Carth reached for the knife and paused at the intersection. Standing behind the wall, she reached for the shadows, cloaking herself. Each time she did it, it became easier, so that now she managed to cloak herself quickly.

Leaning forward, she peered around the corner.

Two men stood with their backs to her, and a young girl was clutched between them.

Living along the docks, she'd seen men like them before. Thevers.

Why were they taking a girl?

"Get her moving so we can get back to drinkin'. Tom wants to ship out in the morning."

They started down the street, dragging the girl with them as they went.

Carth stood watching. The girl fought, but there was only so much she could do to get free. The men holding on to her were bigger than her, and much stronger. The poor girl wouldn't be able to free herself.

Carth squeezed the knife as anger roiled within her. She was to meet Jhon, but she couldn't do nothing, not if this girl was in danger. Jhon would understand.

As she stepped into the street, she tried to hold on to the shadows, wishing she had greater control over them. She stayed near the edge of the buildings, moving as quietly as she could, giving enough distance that she could track them, but not so much that they got too far ahead of her. It was a difficult balance.

The men turned down Doland Street, making their way toward the docks.

At this time of night, the streets were mostly empty. A man passing by turned away, hurrying down an alley as if he wanted nothing to do with what happened here. For the first time since she'd been in Nyaesh, she wished for A'ras involvement. They might attack her, but they also managed to keep the peace.

If the men reached River Road, there would be little that Carth could do, especially if they reached one of the ships docked there. Her best chance of doing anything was now, before they got too far.

Taking a deep breath, she tried cloaking herself in shadows, pulling them around her, and then hurried down the street. Her steps were muted, as if she managed to hang on to part of the shadow cloaking, giving her some silence that protected her.

When she was nearly to the men, one of them started to turn.

Carth stabbed with the knife, catching him in the back of the shoulder before he could turn all the way around.

He screamed. It was a high-pitched sound and full of agony.

Carth almost lost her nerve.

The other man jerked on the girl and started running, leaving his partner writhing on the street. Carth glanced at him, noting that the arm she'd stabbed had blackened, then sprinted after the girl.

They reached River Road before her.

Carth barreled onto the street, trying to stay near the shadows, having the advantage of knowing this part of the city well and knowing where the darkness was deepest.

The man tried hurrying, but now that it was only him with the girl, she was able to fight. She struggled, but then he threw her over his shoulder and ran.

Carth wasn't as tall as him and didn't have the same length that he had, but she was quick, and she could duck between the other people on the street, people he was forced to weave around.

He reached one of the docks.

Carth had to act now. If she didn't, and if he reached the long ship tied to the dock, she doubted she would be able to do anything to save the girl.

She needed a way to distract him and slow him.

"Hey! That's my sister!" she shouted.

She doubted something so simple as that would get him to turn, but it did slow him.

That was enough.

Carth leapt. In her anger and fear, and with the shadows all around, she sailed across the distance, traveling much farther than she normally would.

She landed too close to him. The man took one look at her and swung his fist.

Carth ducked while at the same time stabbing upward. She caught him in the stomach and rolled out of the way.

If the injury was anything like the others, she would see him fall quickly.

The man gasped.

Rather than dropping the girl as Carth had hoped, he staggered down the dock.

Carth chased him and jabbed him with the knife again, this time in the leg. "Just let her go!" she told him. That was all she wanted. If the man would let the girl go, then she would leave him alone. She didn't *want* to hurt him.

He ignored her pleas and limped down the dock. Near the ship, a lantern blinked on. Three men stood watching. The moment they came this way, Carth would have failed.

Water lapped at the dock, swirling around it.

The men started toward her.

Carth did the last thing that she could think of: she rammed into the man, sending him toppling into the river.

She went with him, and her breath burst away when she

hit the cold water. Now it was twice that she'd been in the river, only this time, it was about more than saving her friend's life. She needed to get the girl free of her attacker, and they both needed to get out of the river.

The man had released her as soon as he'd hit the water.

Carth swam toward the girl. She didn't move, and for all she knew, the girl didn't live. As she swam, the man grabbed at her ankle. Kicking herself free, she looked back to see him sinking beneath the surface.

Where was the girl?

The night was too dark to search easily. Had she made a mistake? Would the girl die because of her? The river was a fast-moving sheet of darkness, and they rushed down the shore. She bounced off a rock and bit back the cry that came to her lips.

Trying to swim backward, she heard the sounds of water splashing, but it seemed like it came from far away.

Carth kicked at the water, swimming as quickly as she could in that direction. She neared and saw that the girl struggled to stay above the surface of the water. When she reached her, Carth slipped her arm around her waist.

The girl thrashed with a wild energy. One hand slapped Carth's face, leaving stars flashing in her eyes.

"Let me help you! I'm the one who tried to save you," Carth said. "Can you swim?"

The girl stopped kicking and shook her head. Dark hair hung in her face, but what she could see told her that the girl had been struck. Bruises streaked up the side of her cheek, reminding her of those Kel had worn after being attacked by the man he'd tried stealing from.

"Can you?" the girl asked in a whisper.

"We'll see."

As she angled them toward the shore, she heard another sound in the water, one of a steady slapping. She looked over her shoulder and realized that a small rowboat sliced through the water, coming straight toward them. A lighted lantern in the bow made her think it was the men she'd seen on the dock.

"They'll get me!" the girl said.

Carth swallowed. She couldn't outswim the boat. The shore was nearly ten yards away, and rocky. Even if she could swim fast enough, she would need to be careful around the rocks to keep from getting thrown into them and crushed. So would the boat, but she suspected whoever rowed it had experience around rocks.

Could she cloak her and the girl in shadows as they floated here?

She had to try.

There was no real edge to the darkness. Here it was all around... other than the lantern coming toward them. Could she roll in the edge of the light leading from the lantern?

Focusing on the shadows, she sunk into the darkness, rolling it up and toward her.

Sounds became muted. The light from the lantern on the boat dimmed. The splashing of water along the rocks softened as well. There was only the pounding of her heart, and that felt distant as well.

The girl started to say something, but Carth clamped a

hand over her mouth, silencing her. Waving a finger to shush her, she pointed to the boat.

The girl watched with wide eyes, but remained silent.

They floated, but Carth was able to hold on to the shadows as they did. Were it only so easy on the street.

The rowboat drifted past. One of the men on the boat held the lantern over the edge. They had to be only a few feet away and the lantern swept over their heads, but they continued on, swinging the lantern back in a different direction, now away from them.

Carth sighed. It had worked.

She hadn't been sure it would, especially with them coming so close, but she and the girl had remained hidden even as the small boat passed them. Now she had to get them out of the water.

She didn't want to release her hold on the shadows, fearing that if she did, the rowboat would see them. Instead, she kicked, losing her connection to the shadows for a moment, and then grabbing onto it again. The kick sent her smacking into a sunken rock and she winced again. The next kick got them close enough to the shore that she could see the outline of the rock. One more and she reached the shore, holding steady while the girl climbed to safety.

Carth followed her and sunk next to her, water streaming from her cloak.

The girl watched her, eyes still wide. "Who are you?" she asked.

Carth breathed out shakily. How could she answer when she didn't really know who she was anymore?

Chapter 19

The inside of the tavern was warm, and the hubbub from earlier in the night finally settled, leaving a minstrel playing quietly near the back of the tavern and a few intoxicated patrons slumped over tables. Vera moved between the tables, clearing off plates and mugs and carrying them to the kitchen. Kel helped, staying close by her side. Etan was nowhere to be seen.

"What do you mean you found her?" Hal asked.

Carth nodded to the girl huddled near the hearth. She hadn't moved since Carth had brought her in and set her by the fire for warmth. "I found her."

"Carth," Hal started, "you can't simply bring a girl here like this. It's dangerous for her."

Carth doubted it was dangerous. If *she* could be here, then the girl could be as well. "She needed help."

"Then we'll see her to her family."

"What if she doesn't have any family?" Carth asked. "What if she's a stray like us?"

The girl hadn't really said anything either. Carth wanted

to know why the men had grabbed her and where they were taking her, but hadn't gotten answers yet.

"Not everyone is a stray," Hal said. "Even when they look to be a stray."

"What if she is? Can we not help her? I think the Thevers—"

Vera shot her a hard look, getting her to cut off.

"Why do you think she needs help?" When she didn't answer, Hal pressed. "Carth, why do you think she needs help?"

She told him about the men carrying the girl along the street. She didn't tell Hal that she had stabbed them with an A'ras knife. That would open her up to more questions that she didn't want to answer. She ended by telling him that she had crashed into one of the men and they had tumbled into the river. It made no sense not telling the truth there, especially since they were both still soaked.

Hal shook his head, his brow knitting together in a worried expression. "This isn't our business, Carth. You've intervened in something you shouldn't have. Ahhh…" He started pacing, glancing at the girl every so often. "Damn it. Now we're not safe even here."

"Why? What is it they wanted her for?"

Hal shook his head. "It doesn't matter."

"It matters!" Carth spoke more loudly than she intended. The girl turned toward her, making the most movement she had since getting rescued and coming to the tavern. Lowering her voice, she caught Hal's attention. "Is that why you took us in?"

Hal flushed. "What? No! Nothing like that."

"Like what? What did they want her for?"

Hal sighed, pulled a stool out from one of the tables, and sat heavily on it. "We've taken you in to keep you safe," he said.

"That's what you claim, but how do we know that's what you intend?"

Hal's face looked hurt. "We have done nothing other than feed you and give you a place to live," he said. "We've kept you *from* men like that!"

Carth looked down, feeling ashamed she had said something that hurt Hal. They hadn't been anything but welcoming, a family of sorts, if not the one she wanted. They *had* taken her in when she had no place to go. They did provide food for her. What did they ask in return?

"I'm sorry, Hal," she said. "I shouldn't speak like that. It's just… it's just that I've seen things." She said it in a rush, afraid that Hal would question what she had seen, and how she had seen it. "I've never told you what happened to my parents—"

"You don't have to. Vera and me, well, we saw the way you looked when you returned that first night. We knew something must have happened. There's enough darkness in this world that we didn't want to force you to relive it."

In some ways, that was the kindest thing she'd ever been told. In others, it reminded her of the fact that she had now become a part of that darkness. What else could she be when she used an A'ras knife to stab a man, turning his skin black? What else could she be when she forced a man into the river, where he would drown? What else could she be when all she wanted was revenge for what happened to her mother and father?

"Why would someone try to take her?" she asked Hal.

He looked over at the girl. "This is a dangerous time, Carth. Reshian and A'ras fighting... leaves children without homes."

"What kind of children?" Carth asked. When Hal didn't answer, she pressed. "What kind? Not A'ras, because they'd have homes here." She looked at Kel and her eyes widened. "You're taking in *Reshian* strays?"

Hal sniffed. "The children we've taken in have done nothing wrong. They've lost their home no different than—" He shook his head when Vera shot him a hard glare. "Don't matter now. We help those we can. Move them on to family if they got some. Otherwise keep them from Thevers. They'd move them south, sell them if they could."

"Sell them?"

Hal sighed. "It's happened before."

"Like Gustan?" she asked, thinking of the name of the boy who had been here before she came.

Hal nodded. "Like Gustan."

"What about those without family?"

"We do what we can, Carth."

"Won't A'ras come after them?"

"That's why we pay the Thevers. Gives you some protection from both." He raised his hands to silence her. "This is something beyond you, Carth. You're too young to understand, and pray that you don't—that you won't—understand."

Carth studied the girl huddled near the hearth, wondering what Hal wasn't telling her. "Can she stay for tonight?" Carth asked.

Hal nodded. "Not going to kick her out tonight. Tomorrow we'll have to figure out what will happen. Now I've gotta look for her family, see what I can learn."

He stood and made his way into the kitchen. Carth watched him for a moment. She walked over to the girl and sat next to her, letting the warmth of the fire push the chill from the night and the dampness of the river from her.

"What's your name?" Carth asked.

The girl tensed. "Taryn."

"I'm Carth."

Taryn looked over to her. Her eyes were deep hollows and carried a haunted expression. "Thank you."

"Why were they after you?"

Taryn shook her head. "I don't know."

Carth didn't know how to ask the next question delicately, but she needed to ask it. "What of your family?"

Taryn blinked and turned back to the fire, all the answer that Carth needed. Her family was gone, making her a stray, much like Carth. Why would the men have been after her? Why would they have brought her to the ship?

"What happened to them?" Carth asked.

"They were... they were at the Laseer Festival. There was an attack. They were caught in it."

The Laseer Festival. That couldn't be a coincidence that Taryn's parents had been lost the night that Carth had gone and attempted to sneak into the palace. The same night when the A'ras had nearly killed her.

"What kind of attack?" Carth asked, feeling a sickening sensation in her stomach. Was it her fault that Taryn's family had been lost?

Taryn shook her head. "They found out we'd snuck into the city. All we wanted was a safe place, but... but... there's no safe place," she sobbed.

Carth looked at the ground. That no one would talk about it made it even more likely that it was the A'ras. And the fact that the attack had occurred when she had been there made her worry that she was somehow responsible.

What could she say to Taryn? Nothing that would put her at ease, and nothing that would make any difference. If the A'ras had killed Taryn's parents, and if Carth was in part responsible, there would be nothing for her to say.

"You can stay here tonight," she said.

Taryn looked around the tavern. "I... I don't think that I can stay here."

"Do you have someplace else that you can go?"

Taryn studied her hands. "There is nowhere else."

That had been Carth's fear. "Then you will stay here. The bed is comfortable enough, and the food is good. We'll keep you safe."

Taryn looked up, hope mixed with the tears that welled in her eyes. "For how long?"

How long? Hal didn't want her to stay for long, afraid that she'd been claimed by someone else, but Carth wasn't willing to leave Taryn to get kicked back out on the street, especially not after everything she had gone through to ensure that the girl would be safe.

"As long as it takes."

———————————

After she got Taryn situated, Carth snuck back onto the street. She should just go to bed, worry tomorrow about what else she could do to help Taryn, but she was supposed to have met with Jhon. She didn't want him to have come for her and for her not to have shown.

As she slipped out the hall and into the alley leading out to the street, Kel caught her. He approached hesitantly, as if he wanted to come closer but didn't dare.

"Vera is upset that you brought her here," Kel said.

Carth didn't turn around. "I thought they collected strays."

"They do, but this is different. I'm not sure why, but they are both upset."

"You don't know what it took to help her," Carth said.

Kel took a step toward her. She heard his footsteps on the cobbles without turning. "I saw you."

Carth tensed. "What do you mean, you saw me?"

"On the street. When you chased that man. You stabbed him. I saw it."

Carth swore under her breath. If Kel had seen, then he might say something to Vera and Hal. Then would they allow her to remain? She didn't love the fact that she was here, and that she had no place else to go, but if that was taken from her, she really wouldn't have anywhere. She truly would be a stray.

"You did the same with the man who attacked me," Kel said. He took another step toward her. "You have a knife. A strange one."

Carth turned to face him. "What are you getting at, Kel?"

"Why did you save her?"

"The same reason I saved you."

"I don't think so. You helped me because you know me. You don't know that girl. What would make you risk yourself to help her?"

Carth had asked herself the same thing. Why would she risk herself? It wasn't that she knew the girl. Not like when she'd helped Kel. This had come from a sense that she had to do something. She hadn't been able to stand around, not like everyone else had done. Not only with her, or even with her mother, letting them suffer when intervention would have made a difference, but with Kel and how the man had simply thought to harm him. So many had a chance to intervene but never did, and when she had seen the way Taryn was harmed, dragged down the street, she hadn't had any choice but to get involved.

And wasn't that what Vera and Hal did?

More than anything, that seemed to be the lesson they taught. Hal hadn't needed to get involved when he'd discovered her the day her parents had died, but he had. No one else had done anything. Had he not, what would she have done? She would have gone back to her home, likely waited for her father, and then when he didn't appear, what would she have done?

"Because I had to," she finally answered. "It was what Hal would have done."

"Hal's afraid that you brought her."

Carth nodded. "Maybe he is now, but he would have helped her too."

Kel studied her before taking a step toward her. She turned, unwilling to listen while he berated her more. Taryn was safe. That was enough for now. Whatever Hal feared, whatever reason prevented him from wanting to help when he knew that he should, she had to discover.

"Where are you going?" Kel called after her as she reached the end of the alley.

"I don't know."

Chapter 20

Carth didn't find Jhon at the meeting place that night, or the next night either. By the third night, when he still hadn't shown, she began to wonder if he'd decided against helping her. During that time, she had a growing worry about the activity near the docks, and whether the Thevers would come to blows with the A'ras again.

The days were filled with working with Taryn. Hal disappeared each day, likely to search for Taryn's family, but allowed her to remain with them as he searched. Like Carth, she took the top bunk, making the room full again.

Kel worked with Taryn, teaching her the bump and lift, demonstrating how to collect scraps with something bordering on excitement, an emotion that he'd never shown when it had been Carth. A part of her felt jealous, but then, Taryn was only with them because she had intervened. She wanted Taryn to be accepted.

Etan remained distant. Each day, he disappeared for hours at a time, something he never had done before, appearing late in the day with enough scraps to appease

Vera. Neither Vera nor Hal ever questioned where he disappeared to, almost as if they didn't want to know. Etan became more distant with them, even when he was there. The quiet anger that had always simmered beneath the surface came forward more often, leaving him lashing out at times, yelling or sulking. Surprisingly, Kel was the victim of most of the outbursts, not Carth any longer. That only served to drive an even greater wedge between Carth and Kel, and in the short time Taryn had been with them, Kel had taken to spending much of his free time with her. Every so often, she caught sight of him, and more than once she thought he was with men she knew to be Thevers, but could never quite be certain.

Carth had worried about the repercussions of having Taryn with them, wondering if the men after her—likely Thevers—would discover that she'd been kept so close to the docks, but the ship she'd been brought to had sailed the next morning, leaving nothing but an empty dock and a few stacked crates. Carth felt relief to see that the ship had left, and that only increased the longer they went with nothing more coming of it.

"Why do we need to give part of this to Vera?" Carth overheard Taryn asking.

Kel flashed a smile. "We got to pay our part for the room and the food. Either this or we sell her breads." He pointed to a stack of sweetbread that Taryn hadn't managed to sell.

"But she owns the tavern. Doesn't she have enough?"

Kel shrugged. "She doesn't ask much, so we do what we can," he said. "Besides, it can be kind of fun for us to collect, you know? Take the time to gather a few extra coins, and then you can buy yourself something."

Taryn smiled. "I never see Carth collecting scraps. Doesn't she have to give some to Vera as well?"

Kel shot Carth a look that seemed to warn her off answering.

She pulled her coin purse from her pocket and shook it, jingling the coins within. "I collected already."

Carth didn't have to collect every day, choosing her targets more carefully now. If anything, that drove an even greater distance between her and Kel. He didn't have the luxury of collecting only when he wanted to.

Instead of collecting scraps, Carth remained in the darkness of the alleys, trying to cloak herself, practicing using the shadows during the daytime. It wasn't as easy in the daylight, or as effective. Better, then, to sneak quietly as her father had taught her.

Then at night, she continued to work on trying to move as she held on to her shadow cloak, but so far had not managed to do it any more effectively than she had before. The only time she'd come close was when she had been in the river, floating with the current, but then she hadn't needed to be the one to move. She needed to master it if she was going to find out what Jhon knew of her parents.

Carth made her way toward the docks. Since she'd brought Taryn to the Lyre, Hal had been off. Almost agitated, but that didn't seem quite right. Jumpy. Whatever it was he hadn't shared with her bothered him.

With her ability with shadows, she decided to find out

the answers on her own. The ship where the men had tried taking Taryn might be gone, but there were others like it, and other Thevers, men like those who had attempted to drag her away. Carth didn't need to attack someone to discover answers. All she needed was to stay in the shadows and listen.

As darkness fell, she moved slowly along the street. A girl like herself would be out of place at this time of night, but she stayed toward the edge of buildings as she carefully moved forward, using the techniques her parents had taught her about moving silently.

No sudden movements. Avoid bright light. Wear dark-colored clothing. All of those were lessons she had taken from her father. When she had done each of those things, she still hadn't managed to follow her father. Now that she knew about her ability with shadows, she wondered if he had something similar. Was that the reason he'd pushed her as hard as he had?

Now she would never know. In some ways, not knowing that part of her father hurt more than losing him.

Carth leaned against the wall of one of the warehouses lining the street. A wide doorway created even deeper shadows near her, but she wasn't willing to risk someone seeing her if they came out the doorway. Standing at the edge of the building would be hidden enough.

From here, she could see the street and watch the ships tied to the docks. A few had lanterns lit, pale light drifting through the portholes. Shadows occasionally moved in front of them, but then disappeared again. Other ships were completely darkened. At first, she focused on the ships where she saw light and movement, but she wondered if she shouldn't be watching the ships where she saw nothing. Hadn't the ship that had wanted to claim Taryn been shaded?

Carth waited, not moving, the cloak of shadows pulled around her, keeping her obscured from anyone passing by. There was a strange, muted sense when she stayed in the shadows like this, one that did not prevent her from hearing footsteps across the stones, or the sound of the water as it rushed along the shore, but somehow made sounds that didn't belong stand out.

Movement on one of the ships caught her attention.

No lanterns lit the ship, and she saw nothing at first other than the outline of the vessel. The darkness around it made it difficult to determine what else there might be. Then a shadow moved nearby as the smugglers moved cargo onto the deck.

Curiosity made her bold.

Carth drew the shadows around her, pulling the cloak of shadows as much as she could. As she did, the darkness around the ship eased, almost as if drawing the shadows away made it easier for her to see. The outline of two men stood on the deck of the ship.

Had they been there before?

She couldn't tell. The longer she stared, the clearer it became that there was something other than the two men on the ship, though Carth couldn't see it well, even as the shadows receded.

What she wanted was to cross the street and get closer, but doing so risked exposing her. When she learned to hide within the shadows and still move, she wouldn't have to worry quite as much, but that was a part of her ability she hadn't discovered yet. Maybe it wasn't possible, though Jhon had alluded to the fact that it was.

Instead, she had to release the shadows, if only briefly. Doing so put her at risk, but if she wanted to see what else might be across the street, she would have to take that risk.

The need to understand why the men had grabbed Taryn pushed her. There was something about that she didn't understand, the same reason Hal protected them, risking himself searching for families for the strays.

She let go of the shadows.

They drifted away from her, easing slowly.

Carth trailed the departing darkness, staying as much within it as she could. She crossed the street, keeping pace with the darkness, pausing long enough to pull on the cloak of shadows. When she released it again, she followed it onto the dock, finally stopping next to the ship.

As she stood here, she pulled at the edge of shadows again. In moments, they swirled around her. A moment of concern for whether she was where she should be struck her, and words that Jhon had said to her during one of their sessions resonated in her mind, similar to lessons her father had taught. *There is an art to the darkness. Shadows cannot be where they should not be.*

Had she created shadows that were where they should not be? She didn't think so. Alongside the ship where she stood, shadows naturally trailed away, stretching not only out onto the dock, but around the water as well. It was something she had to think about, not wanting to risk making herself more visible.

Muted voices came from the deck of the ship.

"When do you think he'll come?" Carth heard. The man's voice was harsh and had an accent that made it seem like he came from the north.

"Said it would be tonight."

"That doesn't give us much time."

"Time enough. You know what happened with that last crew."

"They failed. That's on them."

There came the sound of boots softly stepping across wood. "That's not what I heard. I heard the A'ras caught them."

"Careful using that word," the other man said.

"You're as bad as the locals."

"Only because I've seen what they do."

Carth wanted to see the men, wishing she could somehow get a different vantage, but that would require climbing onto the ship. Risking herself by coming this close was bad enough. Attempting to climb on board would be true folly.

"They don't worry about the A'ras, so I don't either."

Something pressed on her, as if trying to separate her from the darkness. Carth backed up to the edge of the dock, her heels hanging almost over the edge, where she could practically feel the wood of the ship behind her. Another step and she might fall into the water. Natural shadows surrounded her, and she used these to draw even more darkness around her.

"You should worry about more than the A'ras."

This was a new voice, distracting her from the strange sense she had of the shadows failing her.

Boots scuffed across the deck and then stopped. "You're early," the northerner said.

"I am when I am." The newcomer had a cold tone to his voice, and something about it seemed familiar, though Carth didn't know why that should be.

"We didn't mean—"

"I don't care what you meant, but you would be foolish to dismiss the A'ras so easily. The Hjan do not."

"We weren't saying that they—"

Carth felt more pressure on the shadows, and the protection around her parted. She felt it disappear with a sudden rush, leaving her standing only in the natural shadows without the benefit of the cloak.

What happened? Was there a limit to how long she could hold on to the shadows? She hadn't detected any before, but that didn't mean that one didn't exist. When she'd used the shadows, the biggest struggle had been simply gathering them to her, creating the cloak. Now that she'd grown more comfortable with it, that process had become easier for her.

"What happened the other night?" the northerner asked.

"We are still trying to determine that."

"You don't know? Thought it was the damn A'ras."

"Ranud…"

"What?" the northerner—Ranud—asked. "Can't keep

up this smuggling if they're gonna get so close. We need to know what we're facing, even if it's something as simple as an accident."

"It ain't no accident. You saw what happened to his arm."

Carth tensed. They were talking about the man she'd stabbed in the arm when she'd rescued Taryn, his flesh turning black from the poison on the knife.

"That was not an accident, but it is not clear whether the A'ras attacked, either. They have been limited from this part of the city, as we agreed."

Limited?

She crept along the side of the ship, knowing that she shouldn't. Even walking here put her at risk of exposure. It would be bad enough were the men to reach her, but if the other man—one who spoke easily about the A'ras, as if unconcerned about their presence—caught her...

There weren't many that she'd met who were unconcerned by the A'ras. Jhon and the others like him were not. The man she'd seen when her mother was killed. That was it. She still hadn't discovered whether Jhon was with Felyn or whether he was only with the man who had grabbed her that day.

A slender ladder led up to the deck. Carth grabbed one of the lower rungs and pulled herself up, listening for the voices of the men on the ship as she did. They were still there, but distantly, although not muted as they had been when she was shrouded. Strange that she actually seemed to hear them better when she used the shadows.

When she neared the railing, she hesitated. She didn't want to risk being seen here. Carth searched for the edge of shadows and found it far from her, nearly to the street, and used that sense to pull it toward her, wrapping herself as much as she could in the shroud.

The effort in doing that was much more than usual.

Carth continued to pull, for the first time feeling the effort of straining at it. Spots formed in her vision, and when the shadows came free, she almost let out a soft gasp, tearing the shadows into her.

Darkness surrounded her.

It came on suddenly, and so fully that she knew immediately that she'd made a mistake. The muted voices sounded suddenly closer, and she heard the newcomer speaking to the others, but he cut off before she could determine what he'd been saying.

Carth froze, holding on to the shadows.

A pressure built on her, and she knew she'd pulled too hard. She felt her grip on the shadows begin to slip, growing weaker the longer she stood there. Carth didn't even trust herself to remain on the ladder without falling. There was no way she could attempt to climb onto the ship, not without being seen by the three men.

Footsteps thudded toward her.

Carth felt her grip on the shadows slip.

She released it and hurried down the ladder.

Reaching the dock, she raced toward the street, berating herself for even attempting to discover what those men were up to.

The problem was, she had learned there *was* something going on, only she hadn't been able to discover what exactly that it was. Worse, they knew she had been there.

Chapter 21

Carth sat away from a lamppost, holding the shadow cloak around her. If she could come up with a way to do it the same as she had in the river, she might be able to move while holding onto it. Then she wouldn't have to fear moving at night at all. Maybe there was something to the way she had floated while in the river, but how could she replicate that on land?

As she pulled on the shadow cloaking, she felt resistance, and a shiver worked along her spine.

Carth leaped to her feet and ducked back into a nearby alley, pulling on the cloaking again. There was resistance there, but not the same as before, and she managed to pull it around her, shrouding herself in the night.

Had the A'ras detected her?

If they had, and if there was some way for them to track her by her use of the shadows, then she needed to be much more careful than she knew. If that was possible, why wouldn't Jhon have warned her?

Unless he didn't know. Even Jhon had admitted to her

that he was not shadow blessed. Without that, what could he really do to help her understand what she could do with this ability?

Carth waited, afraid that whoever had detected her manipulating the shadows knew that she was here, but nothing else came. There was no sense of energy in the air, no sense of her skin growing tight, and not even that itching along her spine that told her someone watched her.

Forcing herself to relax, she released her grip on the shadow cloaking.

It had to be well after midnight. Long since time for her to return to the tavern, and her bed, so that she could actually get enough sleep. The past few days, she had stayed out too late and then been awoken early in the morning by Etan bumping the bunk or by Kel and Taryn chatting excitedly. Maybe it was only fatigue that she felt tonight.

"You should be more careful."

Carth spun, pulling the knife from her pocket. She relaxed when she saw Jhon. "You haven't come back for days. After what happened—"

"I know what happened. The Thevers are of no concern of mine."

Carth took a step back. "They concern *me*."

"I thought you wanted to know about your parents."

"I do, but I thought you'd have done more to tell me. Instead you keep it secret, making me wait to know what you want with my shadow ability!"

"I have certain responsibilities, Carth of Ih-lash."

"You could have sent word."

He nodded, motioning for her to follow him deeper into the alley. Had it been him that she'd detected? She hadn't thought so, but the strange sense had appeared—and disappeared—about the same time he had come. "I could have sent word, but that would mean that you think I am beholden to you in some way."

"You agreed to work with me."

"I did."

"How can you work with me if you're not here?"

"You've been practicing. You don't need me for that part of your training."

He stopped near a wall at the back of the alley. Jhon waved his hand over the wall, but she couldn't tell if he touched anything. A door opened with a soft click, and he motioned her to go through.

"Where are you taking me?" she asked.

"First you question why I haven't been available to instruct you, and now you question how I will instruct you?"

Carth didn't want to argue with him, but at the same time, she felt she had been through enough that she deserved some answers. "I question where you're taking me. That's all."

"Good. Now come with me."

Jhon stepped through the wall. Carth glanced behind her and attempted to pull at the shadows, cloaking herself briefly. Mostly she attempted it because a nagging feeling made her question whether she would be able to. There had been resistance against her when she had attempted it before. Would she have the same resistance?

The shadow cloak came to her, but slowly. Not with a resistance so much as it felt almost like when she attempted to pull on the cloaking during the daytime. Under the sunlight, even when she stood in the shade, reaching for it was more difficult. That was what it felt like now.

A crawling sensation ran along her back, up between her shoulder blades, and she shivered.

The shadows clung to her, but she still had the sense that someone watched her. She had thought her ability protected her from others observing her while she was cloaked, but if that wasn't true, she would have to be more careful.

Carth turned away, stepping through the wall. Once she did, Jhon did something and the wall sealed closed again with another click. The pressure on her faded.

She let out a sigh.

They were in a small room. A faded wooden table took up most of the space, and three chairs sat around the table. Another low table ran along the far wall. A lantern rested on the center table, revealing books and vials stacked beside it. Another door on the far side of the room was closed.

Carth took a seat in one of the chairs and slouched back, letting out another sigh, this time relieved. She'd been searching for Jhon the last few days, and had worried that he had given up on working with her. Finding him again took away that worry but left her with other questions that she wanted answered.

Jhon watched her. "What is it?"

"Tired. That's all."

"Tired?"

Carth nodded. "I think I've been pushing myself too much with shrouding. It's making me tired."

"It wouldn't do that."

"What do you mean? When I attempt to use a shadow cloak, most of the time I can, but sometimes I find that it's just too much work and I can't hold on to the shadows."

Jhon frowned at her for a moment and then shook his head. "Perhaps that is all it is. I will have to check with…" He trailed off before mentioning who he would ask. "You have felt this before?"

She nodded. "I've been practicing."

"I can see that. You're more skilled than the last time I saw you."

"That was only a few days ago."

Jhon stood behind one of the chairs and tapped the top of it. "Indeed. Something has happened that you do not want to share."

Carth sighed and told him about the men abducting Taryn, sharing what had happened to the one attacker's arm when she'd stabbed him with the knife.

Jhon watched her with a concerned expression on his face. "You should not have been able to use the knife in such a way."

Carth pulled the knife from her pocket and set it on the table. "It's a knife. You stab with it."

Jhon stared at the knife. "What you describe is using the magic through the blade. That is what is unexpected."

"I didn't use the magic through the blade. And didn't you say they're poisoned?"

Jhon reached for the knife and lifted it more gingerly than Carth had since she had started carrying it. "The A'ras layer poison atop their swords and their knives, but this isn't poisoned in that manner."

Carth watched him. She hadn't done anything with the knife, only stabbed the attacker. "Then there was no magic through the blade."

Jhon considered her for a moment before handing the knife back. "Have you ever had a similar experience when you've used the knife?"

She thought back to the other times that she had flashed the knife. Not enough to know with certainty. "Maybe once, but I thought you said the blade was poisoned."

"There is poison on an A'ras blade, but that is not what makes it powerful. It is the A'ras magic that does."

"What is the A'ras magic?"

Jhon leaned forward, crossing his arms. "That is something that we have never understood."

"We?"

Jhon met her eyes. "There are those who study, who seek knowledge. The A'ras are enabled in ways that we don't fully understand."

"Why do they want children?"

"What?"

"There was a girl I rescued when I stabbed the man. There are others as well. What are they after with them?"

Jhon stared at the knife before standing. He started pacing, tracing a small circuit through the room. "Children?"

"They go missing. Vera and Hal help the Reshian, but

they don't want to help all the strays." It had taken Carth's insistence to convince them to help Taryn.

Jhon sighed. "Is that why they have come?"

"Why who have come?"

"It would make sense. They would claim them early, and then they could use them, but why here?" Jhon spoke to himself, ignoring the way Carth stared at him. "What do they seek to know?"

"What are you talking about?" she asked him.

Jhon stopped pacing. "Where did you see this?"

"Near the docks. They're fighting with the Thevers for them."

Jhon frowned. "They wouldn't fight the Thevers. They would care little about them."

"I don't understand. Who are you talking about? Why is that important?"

Jhon closed his eyes and his frown deepened. "Can you show me where?"

"I think so."

"Can you shroud us?"

Carth bit her lip and thought of the last time she had been at the docks. The shadow cloaking had worked at first, but then it had faded as she became fatigued. If Jhon needed something longer lasting than that, then she wouldn't be of much help. Would she have to hold the shroud while moving, or would she be able to release it while sneaking along the street?

"I can try, but I don't know how long I can hold it."

Jhon nodded. "It will have to be enough. Are you ready?"

"Ready for what?" she asked. "What lesson are you going to teach me?"

"Movement," he said.

"I can't. I've tried…"

Jhon smiled and patted her on the shoulder. "We will try again. I have faith in you, Carth of Ih-lash. You are one of the shadow blessed. And if you want answers about your parents, and maybe to help others like you, then you must do this for me."

Chapter 22

The night pressed around her, almost a physical presence. When a gust of wind kicked up over the water, sending her heavy cloak fluttering, Carth shivered. Jhon stood unmoving in the shadows near her, shrouded beneath the cloak she'd formed. Within the shadows, she heard his breathing and could practically hear his heartbeat. Why should it be so noticeable?

"When are we going to move?" she asked. It wasn't the question she wanted to ask. She *wanted* him to tell her what he knew about her parents, and why they had been killed, but Jhon had ignored her basic questions. She doubted he'd answer the harder ones.

He shook his head, his gaze fixed on the docks and the ships moored there. When they had arrived, Carth had pointed to the ship where she had detected movement, where she'd heard the northerner and the other men on board the night before. For some reason, the ship interested him.

Carth continued to hold the shrouding, wondering how

long she would be able to cling to it. Jhon seemed convinced she shouldn't have grown as weak as she had, but Carth had felt the way her control over the darkness had faded, weakened no differently than muscles used too long.

Nothing moved on the ship tonight. Lanterns glowed on the neighboring ships, but not on the one they studied. Somehow, she had seen the ship more clearly the last time. What had she done?

There was something about the way she had used the shadows. Could she pull on the cloaking, drawing it to her even more?

Taking in a deep breath, she used the sense of the darkness, feeling it as it wrapped around her. How could she draw it away?

Jhon described it as cloaking, and when she did it, there was a sense that the shadows became something real. Could she *shift* the cloaking somehow?

She pulled.

There were no other words to describe what she attempted, and she grabbed at the air, almost like there was a physical thing that she could touch, and dragged the shadows, swirling them around her.

Jhon looked over at her, his eyes narrowing. "What are you doing?"

She noticed how the shadows eased away, leaving the night lessened somewhat. No longer did the ship appear as gradations of darkness. Now she managed to see the distinct outline of the ship and that nothing moved on the deck.

"Can you see it?" Carth asked.

"I do not need to see it. I can feel it."

"What can you feel?"

"There is power in the air when you use the shadows, much power." Jhon studied her for a moment before turning his attention back to the ship. "As to what I can see… there is nothing but the night."

"I thought that when I pulled the shadows, others could see them."

Jhon glanced in her direction. "As I said, I do not need to see anything to know that you are here. My eyes might not show me anything, but other senses reveal you to me."

"You can't *see* me?"

"You are shadow blessed, Carth. You are shrouded in shadow. That much I know."

"When I wrap myself in the shadows, I can see the ship easier. Like the night disappears."

Jhon frowned. "There are stories of those shadow blessed who can become a part of the darkness itself. A rare ability, perhaps rarer even than the ability that you possess. What is it you see on the ship?"

"Nothing."

Jhon nodded. "Then we go."

He started across the street, not waiting for her. Carth slowly released the shadows, letting them unfurl. As she did, she moved within them. Every few steps, she paused and gathered the darkness back to her before releasing it again, letting it ease away so that she could remain within it.

"You will need to learn caution in using your abilities," Jhon said.

"You said that you can't see me."

"I cannot. But I do not need to see you to know that you are there. I can *feel* you, as would anyone else sensitive to it. Every time you pulse"—he waved his hand up and down as if to emphasize what she did—"I detect it again. There is a signature to it, if you listen."

"Can anyone detect it?" She had thought herself protected by the night, and by the shadows, but if that wasn't true, then her ability would be much less useful than she had thought.

"Only those attuned to such things, and those shadow blessed."

"Like you?"

"As I said, I am not shadow blessed. My ability is with the detection only. It is much like the A'ras. Only another of the A'ras can detect when their magic is used."

Carth released most of the shadows without taking another step. "That's not true. I can tell when the A'ras use their magic."

Jhon frowned and pulled her to the side of the street. "What do you mean?"

"I feel it when the A'ras use their magic. It's like after a lightning strike and my skin gets all tight. I feel it. Is that what you feel when I gather the shadows?"

"No," he said carefully. "When you pull on the shadows, I feel a pulsing within my blood. It is an ability tied to me, and my kind."

"Your kind?"

Jhon nodded without answering. "You should not be

able to detect the A'ras magic. I do not know what it means that you can."

They stood in the shadows off to the side of the street, near a warehouse much like the one where Carth had rescued Jhon, keeping the A'ras from discovering him. Jhon cupped his hands together and brought them to his face, breathing slowly, like a Assage priest meditating. Carth decided not to interrupt, but wondered why she should be able to detect the A'ras magic.

"I think," Jhon began, tearing his eyes off the ship and looking over at her with a blank expression on his face, "that it is time for you to return to the tavern for the night."

She wanted to hide the disappointment she felt. She hadn't found him for three days, and now when she finally did, he wouldn't work with her. What had she said that offended him? "I thought we were going to practice."

"And we did. You demonstrated the strength of your ability. That is enough for tonight." He took her by the elbow and guided her back onto River Street. "You must be careful practicing with the shadows. I had not thought it an issue before tonight, but it is too easy for me to detect when you do. Such a thing places you in danger."

"From the A'ras?"

Jhon shook his head. "There are worse things than the A'ras."

They reached the Wounded Lyre, and Jhon released her elbow. "Remain careful until we meet again."

"I thought you were going to tell me about my parents!"

Jhon's mouth tightened. "It is not what I know about

your parents that's important, but about how they died. And that… that I think is too dangerous to share with you right now, especially with what you have demonstrated. I will continue to look for you as often as I can, but I may not be as available as I have been."

She nodded, wanting to snap at him that he hadn't been available to her the last few days at all, but decided not to risk angering him. "If I can't practice, how will I continue to learn?"

"I did not say not to practice, only to be careful. Practice in the daylight. It will be safer that way."

"There aren't enough shadows in the daytime."

"No? I think you have yet to find the right places. Have you never stood in the shade of a tall tree under the summer sun? Have you never eased against a cool building to relax? There are places of shade even under the brightest sun, Carth Shadow Born. Practice, but do so with caution until I see you next. Hopefully by then I will have the answers I need and we can progress."

"Progress to what?"

"To keeping you safe."

"What about what you wanted my help with?"

"I am no longer certain that is wise."

"But you said you needed me!"

"I was wrong. Be careful, Carth of Ih-lash. I will find you again soon."

He left her and quickly disappeared into the night, heading along the shore, as if leaving the city. Carth watched, tempted to pull away the shadows so that she could watch him go, but decided against it. If he was right, if she could somehow be detected when she used her shadow magic, she shouldn't risk the A'ras—or whatever Jhon thought might be worse—detecting her.

Carth considered returning to the streets, wandering back into the night, but Jhon's words left her concerned. How many nights had she risked herself unnecessarily, thinking herself hidden when she used the shadow cloak, when in reality, she made her presence known to those with the ability to detect it, those who would be dangerous for her to find?

She didn't want even to stand in the shadows now. If she did, would she be able to resist the temptation to pull the cloak?

With a sigh, she entered the tavern.

Lanterns hung from two of the posts, giving some light to the dining portion of the room. A crackling hearth provided additional light and warmth, pushing back the chill she'd felt while out in the night, a chill that her cloak hadn't managed to dispel. She counted seven people still sitting in the tavern, taking up three tables. There was no sign of Kel or Taryn or Etan.

She headed toward the kitchen, wanting to find Vera or Hal. Instead, Etan greeted her on the other side of the door, a dark sneer parting his lips.

"About time you returned," he said.

"What's that supposed to mean? I've collected all the scraps I needed for today."

She hadn't collected anything today, but she still had

enough from a coin purse full of silver that she didn't really have to collect for a while. Etan didn't need to know that, though. For that matter, Kel didn't need to know, and she hadn't told him.

"Means that you've been gone a long time. The others have noticed."

"Kel knows I left."

His sneer faltered a moment. "I'm sure he does. Since you came, you've been pulling him away, haven't you? Now you've even got your new friend working on him. Those of us who used to do fine with our scraps now get nothing. I suppose you had something to do with that, too, didn't you?"

"What are you talking about?"

A thudding of footsteps came from the back hall and Etan glanced over his shoulder. "Doesn't matter. Pretty soon it won't. I've got all the protection I need now."

Etan started past her and she noticed the streaks of wetness down his cheeks. Etan had been crying. She hadn't seen him display any emotion other than his joy when she'd nearly been caught. He had barely expressed any fear when Kel had been hurt, not bothering to ask *why* he hid a bruise. What would make him cry like this now?

"Etan," she said, trying to catch his arm as he reached the door out of the kitchen.

He jerked his arm away. "Best stay back from me. Of course, that won't matter soon, will it?"

"What *are* you talking about? Have you been dipping into Hal's ale?"

He hesitated. She thought he might say something more, but he sniffed and shook his head, pushing out of the kitchen and back into the tavern.

Carth watched the door swing shut before making her way toward their room. A lantern glowed through the cracks in the door, and she pushed it open, wondering why Kel would still be awake. She found him sitting on his bunk, staring blankly.

"What is it, Kel?" she asked.

He didn't move. He didn't even look over at her. His eyes remained fixed straight ahead of him and he stared, unblinking.

Carth closed the door and approached him carefully. "Kel?"

He swung his head to her, his wild hair brushing the top of the bunk—Taryn's bunk—and he blinked, as if seeing her for the first time. "Carth?" His voice came out as a whisper.

"What happened?" She stood on her toes and peeked into Taryn's bunk but found it empty. "Where is Taryn?"

"She's gone," he said.

"What do you mean, she's gone?"

He shifted his focus back to the door, still staring blankly. "They came for her."

Carth's heart sped up. She grabbed Kel's chin and turned him so he met her eyes. "Who? Who came for her?"

"Doesn't matter."

"Yes, it does! You need to tell me what happened!"

"We were… we were in the street. Taryn said we needed to return to the tavern. Insisted on it. I thought she'd made a mistake trying to collect scraps, but she told me she didn't. They followed us here."

"Who followed you?"

"Hal tried to intervene."

A terrible sensation started to rise in her stomach. "What happened to Hal?"

"When he... when he did, they knocked him to the ground with barely more than a flick of their wrist. I've never seen anything like it before."

Kel started trembling and pulled himself away. "You should have been with us, but you left! Always sneaking off into the city. She was your responsibility, Carth!"

Even though she thought she knew what had happened, she still needed him to say it. He had to tell her; otherwise it wasn't real. It couldn't be real.

"Who came to the tavern?" she asked carefully.

Kel turned his focus back to the door. "I don't know. I hid from them."

"But you have an idea, don't you?"

Kel's eyes closed. "I think it was the A'ras, Carth. They attacked Hal and they took Taryn."

Chapter 23

Carth couldn't sit still. She tried resting, but her mind raced. Why would the A'ras have come for Taryn? It had to do with the Reshian and their stupid fight outside the city, didn't it?

Maybe it was something else. Jhon thought there was something to the Thevers smuggling children. Was that tied somehow to the Reshian? Was *that* why the A'ras had come for her?

She hurried through the streets, searching for Jhon.

She hadn't found any sign of Hal—nor of Vera, for that matter. The tavern had been nearly empty by that time, and the street outside desolate. She'd searched along the shore but found no sign of Jhon, which made her change her approach and head into the city.

The A'ras had Taryn.

The girl was her responsibility. Carth had rescued her and had thought that would bring her safety, that Vera and Hal could protect her, but what was protection other than an illusion?

Why did the A'ras keep ruining things in her life? Her

parents first, then chasing her, and now... now Taryn.

Carth wanted answers. No—she wanted revenge, but she doubted even her shadow ability would help with that. First, she needed to find Jhon.

Had she not brought Taryn to the Lyre, Hal would have been unharmed. She didn't need to see him to know that he was dead. Everyone she cared about died, especially when the A'ras got involved. What if the A'ras sliced him with their blade? If that happened, he would be dead. The poison from their magic would have leached into his body and blackened it, the same as had happened to the man Carth had stabbed.

Now she needed to find Taryn. She didn't know what she intended, only that she would find the girl and find some way to bring her back to the tavern. Carth refused to think of what she would do next. There wasn't anything she could do.

The streets were basically empty, and she didn't know where to find the A'ras. She could go to the palace, but there would be too many there for her to do anything. She could sense when the A'ras used their magic. If only she could follow that, she might know whether any of the A'ras were closer than she expected.

Carth stopped. When had she felt it before?

There had been the connection to the shadows. She didn't know if that had been the only time she had detected it, but it seemed like the easiest way to reach for them now.

She moved into an alleyway, away from the street, and pulled on the shadows, cloaking herself in them. She stood, holding on to the darkness, letting the sense of it surround her. If Jhon was right, then she would be noticed doing this. Maybe he would find her as well. That might be the best option, especially if she was to get help reaching Taryn.

As she stood there holding onto the shadows, a steady throbbing slowly began to press against her. At first it was subtle, something she wasn't certain that she detected, but the sensation began to increase, leaving her skin feeling tight and drawn: the distinct sense of the A'ras magic being used.

Could she track using the sense?

The more she focused on it, the more she thought that she might be able to use it. And maybe she would detect the A'ras deeper into the city, thinking they would be nearer the palace. But that wasn't what she detected. This was near the river.

Carth released the connection to the shadows and started back down the street, making her way toward the river. Once there, hiding along the shores, letting the sound of the water roaring along the rocks rush past her, she pulled the shadows toward her again.

With it, she felt the tightening of power against her skin.

Was it near the docks and the ships?

Could she have rescued Taryn from her attackers, only to have her grabbed by the A'ras and brought to the ship anyway?

But she didn't detect them near the ships. It came from somewhere away from the city.

Carth made her way along the rocks, pausing every so often to pull on the shadows, to let the pressure from the magic push against her. As she did, she knew she headed in the right direction. Every few steps, the sense of the magic stretching her skin grew more intense.

She reached the outer edge of the city. The row of taverns and shops along River Road transitioned to ramshackle homes, and then to nothing as Nyaesh ended. The river continued to flow beyond the city, eventually reaching the sea. From here, she could see nothing of what the river would be, or the power it would possess. There was only the emptiness.

Carth paused and pulled on the darkness. There was the sense of power against her, but now it seemed to emanate from deeper in the city again. Had she been mistaken? Had she missed something with the A'ras and somehow followed the wrong path?

She wished Jhon were with her to help guide her, but he wouldn't have allowed her to come with him. He didn't think she should risk herself using the shadow magic, but Carth was meant to learn it. Her father *had* to have been teaching her that, hadn't he? If she was shadow blessed, that meant that she could use the power of the darkness, that it was her birthright. Didn't it?

If only her father were still alive to teach her, to help her to understand why she could manipulate the shadows. Maybe he would have taught her using other games, thinking she would learn to control the darkness the same way she had learned to follow her mother, or find her father when he followed close behind her.

There had been no game of shadows, nothing like the

lessons he had worked on with her. Carth wondered when he would have begun teaching her those lessons—unless he had brought her to Nyaesh to keep her from them.

She followed a narrow path leading along the river. This was where she had detected the A'ras magic, even if she didn't detect it now.

Voices drifted in the night and she froze. Carth considered pulling on the shadows, but decided against it. If Jhon could detect her when she did, others could as well. Rather than using her shadow skills, she crept slowly forward, trying to remain hidden in natural shadows. Moonlight shone brightly overhead, and she wore a gray cloak, one that would better fade into the shadows of the daylight rather than the blackness of night. She feared that the moonlight reflected off her cloak too brightly.

Carth shrugged it off, standing only in her brown dress. This was better, but it was still too obvious. Better than with the cloak, though, and she tucked her braid down the back of her dress, wishing she had nevern oil and choclem leaves like she'd sought when she'd helped Kel mask his bruising. The choclem might be too dark for him—and for her—but it would help obscure her.

The voices came from the other side of a small rise. The land was flat here, with little slope to it, barely enough to prevent anyone from noticing she was here. Were there any rocks, or anything else to hide behind, she might be able to make her way forward, but she had nothing to use.

Only, there was one place she could hide as she made her way toward the voices.

She glanced at the river. It rushed through here more violently than it did near the docks. Massive rocks lined the shore leading down toward the water. She'd been in the river twice before and could have died both times; should she really risk the river a third time?

The sound of the voices came closer.

Carth had to go somewhere. If she stayed here, whoever came along the street would discover her. If she tried racing back to the city, she likely wouldn't make it before whoever was coming discovered her.

As she climbed onto the rocks, she held on carefully. They were massive, and slick with water and algae. Another option came to her. She didn't have to climb into the river, not if she could hide among the rocks. If she was willing to risk it, she could pull on the shadows and hide herself, but she feared someone like Jhon with the ability to detect her using that skill.

As she pressed herself against the rock, she realized her mistake. Her cloak lay on the ground, near the path where she'd shaken it off.

Swearing softly to herself, Carth climbed off the rock and back to the path. She snatched up her cloak and hurried back to the shore, where she slipped as she tried getting back into a hiding place between a pair of enormous slick rocks.

The voices she heard paused.

Had they heard her?

Carth froze, fearing the worst. If they heard her, she might have to shroud herself with shadows to keep safe.

The soft murmuring resumed.

She started along the rock, pulling herself carefully so that she wouldn't make too much noise. She climbed from rock to rock, pausing in the darkest spaces between the rocks and listening before moving on. Eventually, she got close enough that she heard the voices clearly.

"You should be more careful."

Carth recognized Jhon's voice and lowered her head. Would he be angry that she'd followed him here?

"As should you. I am allowed in the city." A woman spoke in a terse fashion. Carth had heard the voice before but didn't know where.

"My presence is tolerated."

"Tolerated is not the same as welcome," the woman said.

Carth wanted to know when she had heard the woman's voice before. Peeking her head above the rock, she saw Jhon walking with the woman. He was dressed the same as when she'd last seen him and stood near a small wooden building that seemed out of place here, beyond the edge of the city.

She glanced back toward the city and realized that it would be difficult—if not impossible—to reach the building other than by climbing the rocks as she did.

The woman had her back to Carth and wore a long, plain cloak. Deep brown or black hair hung in waves beyond her shoulders, tied up with a dark ribbon.

"You know why I came."

"As I said, you should be more careful."

"What of you? Are you careful?" Jhon asked.

"As careful as I can be given the circumstances. You know

as well as I what we face. They have proven more troublesome than we expected."

"Only because you expected nothing," Jhon said.

"There is that."

"I have found one of their men, but not the other."

"You think they have only come in a pair?" the woman asked. She paced slowly back and forth in front of the building before pausing in front of Jhon.

"I would know if there were others."

"I am not convinced that you would," she said.

"Have you discovered anything from the other?"

The woman began pacing again, always managing to stay out of the moonlight. Did she control the shadows the same as Carth? Was that why he had come to her?

"He refuses us so far. That will change."

"Have you discovered how you caught him?" Jhon asked.

That seemed a strange question to ask, but stranger still was the woman's answer.

"We found him on the street, staving off death. We have not discovered the trick of that yet, but we will. Then we will find the other."

"He is more skilled than you can understand."

"Do you think I don't know that?"

The woman started moving again, this time putting more space between herself and Jhon. She made her way toward the river, and still Carth couldn't make out her features, leaving her covered in darkness. As the woman approached, Carth felt a twinge of energy in the air. She'd felt it before, but always when there were A'ras around, and this woman… could she be one of the A'ras?

She continued toward the river.

Carth ducked down, trying to hide herself. Over the sound of water rushing along the river, she heard footsteps. The woman came close.

"They seek to draw those with A'ras ability from the city," Jhon said.

"We would know if that were the case."

"Would you? How many have you lost? They smuggle the Reshian as well, using the guise of common thieves. Had I not seen it myself…"

"What are you getting at?"

"Perhaps nothing. I tracked them here for us to see ourselves."

"That wasn't why you called me here."

"No. There's another reason. You never told me that she was to be tested."

"Would it have mattered?"

"I would have brought her to you. Leaving her along the docks…"

The woman paused and peered into the darkness. Had she seen Carth?

Carth pulled on the shadows, reaching for the barest edge as she sunk into the darkness, trying to hide her entire body not only between the rocks, but also beneath the blanket of shadows.

The sense of energy in the air increased and her skin grew tight.

Carth held her breath. There was no question now that

one of the A'ras was here. Was it the woman? Could Jhon have gone to them? But why?

Then again, what did she really know about Jhon? He had mysterious knowledge and skills, but he hadn't shared anything about himself. Maybe he sided with the A'ras. Yet she had seen him attack the A'ras, hadn't she?

The other possibility, that the A'ras had discovered Jhon, seemed less likely. He would have known, wouldn't he?

"What is it?" Jhon asked. His voice came through to her in a muted fashion, the strange pressure on the air from the cloaking of shadows obscuring it somewhat.

"I feel… something."

"What do you feel?" Jhon asked.

He had approached, making his voice louder, but still muted while Carth hung in the shroud of shadows.

Had the woman detected her using the shadow cloaking?

She eased away some of the shadows, still holding on to them, but with less of a connection than she'd had before. The strange, muted voice changed as well.

The energy in the air increased, and Carth's skin felt stretched even tighter.

Definitely an A'ras.

Why would Jhon be with her?

"Perhaps it was nothing," the woman said.

"What did you feel?" Jhon asked again.

Carth wished she could recede into the depths of the shadows, pulling away from the A'ras and from Jhon, but where would she go other than into the water?

"There was a surge of power. It is gone now."

Carth heard footsteps along the rocks nearest her and recognized them as Jhon's. She tried moving, glancing back to see the dark outline of a boat in the water. As she did, a chill washed over her and then was gone, faded as if nothing more than her imagination.

As it faded, someone grabbed her shoulders and lifted her easily.

Carth resisted the urge to cry out. Doing so would do no good. Then Jhon set her onto the ground facing the A'ras, the same woman who had chased her through the city after she'd found the herbalist shop destroyed. Carth glared at him, unable to believe that he had betrayed her.

Chapter 24

Carth stared at Jhon, who looked at her with an unreadable expression. "Why?" she demanded.

He arched a brow as he frowned. "You shouldn't have come here. If he catches you—"

"This is her?" the A'ras said.

Carth couldn't take her eyes off the A'ras and found her gaze drifting to the slender sword sheathed at her side. Where she'd been, along the water, she hadn't been able to see it, but now... now the blade almost pressed upon her senses.

She resisted the urge to reach for the knife in her pocket.

"This is her," Jhon said.

Carth needed to get away, but Jhon would know, wouldn't he?

Only, there were other things that she'd discovered about her ability.

Reaching for the shadows, she started to sink into them.

The A'ras stepped toward her, reaching for her sword.

Jhon darted toward Carth.

She couldn't wait. As she relaxed into the shadows, she jumped.

The last time she had done the same, she had managed to jump much farther than she'd thought she should. This time, the jump carried her over the A'ras. She cleared the woman's head and landed close to the small wooden building.

Carth ran.

Jhon called after her, but Carth didn't hesitate. Instead, she pulled on the shadows, for the first time feeling them coalesce around her as she moved, managing to maintain the connection as she ran. But it was more than running. She flowed within the shadows, a part of them in some ways. The jump had been a part of the shadows, using the insubstantial power from within the darkness to carry her beyond Jhon and the A'ras.

At the building, she had started to weave around the side when she heard a familiar voice.

"Taryn?" she whispered.

Carth slammed into the door, pressing through it, all while holding on to the darkness. Wrapped as she was in the shadows, she easily kicked the door open and ran into the room.

And froze.

Taryn wasn't the only person here.

Carth lost control of the shadows. They drifted away from her, quickly easing back into the night.

Had Jhon known?

She spun, pulling the knife from her pocket as she faced

the doorway. Jhon stood watching her, the A'ras woman behind him. Carth was surprised to see that her sword remained sheathed.

"Why did you do this?" she whispered to Jhon.

"This is not what you think."

"That's your answer?" Carth snapped. "This isn't what I think? What is it, then?"

Jhon stepped to the side. "This is about why you came to Nyaesh."

"Why I came... I came because my parents brought me here."

"They did," Jhon said.

Carth couldn't take her eyes off the woman. She stood outlined against the night, and Carth realized the ribbon in her hair was the maroon of the A'ras. Her hand rested on the hilt of her sword. "Why would you pretend to help me?"

"I have been helping you," Jhon said.

Carth risked looking over her shoulder at the three children huddled there. Taryn met her eyes, but the others looked away, frightened.

"Helping *me*? It looks like you're doing the same as the others. What is it about the children of the city?"

When she looked back to Jhon, she noted the angry glint in his eyes. He managed to mask his emotions well, so for him to show such emotion made her nervous. "Power converges here, Carthenne, power that many would like to harness. I hadn't known about it until you brought me to the docks. I have you to thank for revealing what they intend."

"You're working with the A'ras!"

"As you would have."

Carth shook her head. "I never would have worked with the A'ras. My parents—"

Jhon's eyes softened, only a little. "Brought you to Nyaesh to work with the A'ras. They were in contact with Avera—"

Carth couldn't stop shaking her head. "The A'ras *killed* my parents!" She held the knife out in front of her and her hand trembled. "I saw what happened to them! I was there when the A'ras killed my mother!"

The woman took a step toward Carth, and Carth jabbed at her with her knife. There was little she could do to protect herself if the A'ras attacked her, but she would try, even if it meant using the A'ras weapon against her.

The woman raised her hands.

Carth froze. Would the A'ras use her magic on her?

"We did not harm your mother," the woman said. "Another did."

"I was *there*!"

"You saw what came after. You were to be tested. Your mother came to us, wanting you trained. After what happened in Ih-lash, and the fighting with Reshian, she wanted you to be trained. But entry to the A'ras is difficult, even for those educated within Nyaesh, and you were an outsider. Few were willing to offer testing; fewer still expected you to pass. She thought to teach you more before the testing."

"No. I saw what happened. I saw my mother—"

"You saw what Felyn did to your mother," Jhon said.

Carth shivered at the mention of his name. Felyn had been there the day her parents were killed—the one who had dispatched three of the A'ras as easily as if they had no magic, and the man Carth had sought for weeks after her parents died, hoping she could ask for his help in getting revenge.

"That wasn't him," she said. "I saw—"

"You saw him attack the A'ras," Jhon said. "Your mother was gone by the time they arrived. He's been working with the Thevers, smuggling those with A'ras potential from the city. You would have been a valuable find."

"Why?" Carth still clutched her knife and held it out, wanting nothing more than to stab the A'ras as she had stabbed the others.

"Because of who you are," the woman said.

"No. I don't believe—"

"There is no believing or disbelieving. Only what happened," the woman said.

Carth shook her head, struggling with what they were telling her. Could her parents really have brought her to Nyaesh so that she could work with the A'ras?

Her father had taught her to fear the A'ras... hadn't he?

Do not let them see you. There is power in hiding. Use the shadows.

His words drifted into her mind as if he were standing right next to her. Would her father have wanted her to work with them?

"Your mother sought our help in your education," the woman went on. "There are many who come thinking that they can learn from the A'ras, but few actually manage it."

Carth looked past the woman and focused on Jhon. "You taught me to hide from them!"

"I helped you find your ability. That is all I did."

"That's not what you did. You showed me how to reach the shadows and how to use that to conceal myself."

"You already knew those tricks. I only allowed you to see the extent of what you were capable of doing. I am not shadow blessed, Carth of Ih-lash. I would not have been able to teach you what you can do, or how to advance your skills, but the A'ras can."

It all still seemed too much. Jhon had helped hide her from the A'ras. He had explained what the A'ras intended, and how they used their magic. Why would he work with them?

She looked back at Taryn. It had to do with her, didn't it? Whatever Jhon wanted had some connection to Taryn. Maybe not only Taryn, but to Stiv, and the others who had gone missing.

"Why do you have her here?" she demanded.

"They would use them," the A'ras said.

"What do you mean?"

"You know what is meant. You have seen him and seen what he is willing to do."

"Felyn?"

"That is the name he uses in these lands."

"Why? What does he want?"

"It is not a what so much as a who. The Hjan will stop at nothing to reach their goal."

"And what goal is that?"

"They want—"

The A'ras spun quickly, cutting off what she might have said.

As she did, Carth felt a strange buildup, a pressure that both reminded her of when the A'ras used their magic and, at the same time, felt completely different.

Shadows swirled into the small room.

"He is here," the A'ras said. She unsheathed her sword and darted into the darkness.

Jhon looked at Carth. "You should not go anywhere."

He followed the A'ras.

The shadows receded from the doorway, like a fog rolling out, leaving the sea.

Carth turned to the others in the room. Taryn had remained silent the entire time, but the others did as well, almost as if they couldn't or weren't allowed to speak.

"Do you know why they took you?" Carth asked Taryn.

She shook her head, looking past Carth and out into the night. She shivered, though it wasn't cold. "They didn't take me. Rescued."

"What do you mean? Kel said the A'ras took you."

"Not them. I was trying to collect scraps. The other boy was there, and then… and then…" She sobbed, rubbing her fist against her eyes to wipe away the tears. "Then cold grabbed me. I couldn't do anything. I was carried off."

"Carried off by what?" If the A'ras and Jhon told the truth—which Carth couldn't believe right now—then it had been Felyn and not the A'ras who had killed her mother.

"Carth?" Taryn said.

Carth focused on the other two with Taryn. They hadn't spoken. Both were much younger than Taryn, reminding her of Stiv.

"Carth!"

"What is it?"

Taryn pointed past her, through the doorway.

Carth followed the direction Taryn's pointing finger. A figure moved, coming closer.

Without thinking too much about it, she pulled on the shadows.

Everything changed. Sounds became more muted, but also heightened in some way. She felt the shroud fall upon her and jumped, leaping into the night toward the figure.

For the first time, she felt a sort of power surge through her. She flowed on this power, letting it carry her. She had done this before, she realized, when she had seen Jhon and the A'ras, but that had been fear driving her. This time... this time, she went out of anger.

Outside the small building, she remained wrapped in the shadows. What she saw nearly made her lose control of her hold.

Etan.

Chapter 25

Carth felt the pressure of power on him, similar to what she felt around the A'ras.

Could Etan be using the A'ras power?

She raced into the darkness after Etan. The air had changed, carrying a hot current of violent energy on it. "What are you doing here?" She released enough of the shadows to reveal herself to Etan.

Etan hesitated. "Carth? You shouldn't be here."

Carth shook her head. "I think the same is true for you."

Another surge in the power filled the air, almost like lightning building during a storm. Her skin drew tight in a rapid fashion.

Carth turned quickly, looking behind her, thinking she would see the A'ras there, but she did not.

A man wearing a plain gray cloak stood facing the door into the small hut.

Carth didn't have to see his face to recognize him. How much time had she spent searching for him, only for him to find her here, of all places?

She started toward him, but Etan grabbed her wrist, pulling her around.

He was stronger than her and bigger, and he forced her to face him. "You go up there and you will die."

She pointed the knife at him. "Is this because of you? Did you bring him here?"

Etan blinked and thrust his chin forward in defiance. "This is your fault. You were the one who brought attention to us. We got along just fine before Hal brought you in. But then you had to go and sneak off with too much. You weren't satisfied with coins."

"I never took anything but scraps."

"Scraps. Some of us want more than scraps. Safety. And the Thevers promised it to me."

"You think that's safety? After what you saw with Stiv? And the boy before me?"

"You can't understand. I'm in with the Thevers now. You can be safe. Let him do what he needs to do and then he'll go. That's what they told me."

"And you believed them?" Carth asked.

"I—"

The A'ras appeared, keeping him from finishing.

She came on a flash of light. Power burst from her with force, sending Felyn sliding across the ground.

He looked over at the A'ras with a lazy smile. "You think to attack me alone?"

"If I must."

Felyn flickered forward. Carth had no other way of describing what she saw. He stood in the doorway, and then he didn't, appearing next to the A'ras.

She swung her sword toward him, but was not fast enough to hit him. Felyn managed to block her sword, doing so with the same laziness as his smile.

"You will fall like the others."

"The Hjan can die too," the A'ras said. "The body we found proved that much."

Felyn's eyes narrowed. "That was not A'ras. That was—"

Jhon appeared.

Carth blinked. He hadn't been there before. How would he suddenly just appear?

"Ah. I understand now," Felyn said. "C'than thinks to intervene. I thought dispatching the last Ih-lash threat would end it." He looked at the A'ras. "As well as others who thought they should intervene. I think I have demonstrated how little the A'ras can do to stop the Hjan."

Carth's heart raced. Felyn *had* attacked her parents.

Hot anger surged through her as she gripped the knife.

Etan grabbed her arm but she shook him off and started forward.

Jhon saw her moving and shook his head.

She ignored him.

This man had killed her parents. Had killed others in the city. She didn't know what he intended with Taryn, but she was tied to it as well. Carth would not let that continue.

Jhon seemed to realize that he would not deter Carth and unsheathed a slender sword that she had never known him to carry.

She began to pull on the shadows, wrapping herself in them.

Etan gasped but she ignored him, letting the darkness surround her.

The A'ras looked over at Carth, eyes narrowing, and then she attacked Felyn.

She moved more quickly than the other A'ras Carth had seen. Power surged with her, filling the air with energy, leaving Carth breathless. Jhon added his attack as well, slashing with his sword, dancing in a way she had only seen from sword masters.

Neither were fast enough.

Felyn struck with a furious violence.

Carth stood frozen. There was nothing she could do to stop Felyn, just as there would have been nothing her parents could have done. This man and his attack were more than any of them could withstand.

Jhon grunted. Blood spilled over his hand where Felyn struck him.

The A'ras pressed forward, but a resigned expression crossed her face.

Carth had to do something. She had her knife, but she also had the shadows, even if she hadn't mastered moving with them.

For her parents, she had to try.

Carth gathered them to her, wrapping herself tightly.

"No," Jhon said as she neared. "Just run. You might be the last—"

His voice came to her as a muted sigh, and she ignored him. She could no more leave than she expected to be able to do anything to stop Felyn.

When the darkness filled her, she released it.

This time, she flowed with it.

Carth held her knife, and when she reached Felyn, she stabbed, pressing all of her anger, all of the darkness that she'd summoned, into the knife and the attack.

It struck his arm, nothing more than a glancing blow.

Felyn turned to her. "Ah... *this* is what I have searched for. I feel it now, the energy you control. It is raw, but..."

He glanced at his arm before looking back at Carth. She'd lost her shadows in the attack, no longer able to hold them and no longer hidden by them.

Felyn swung his sword, but it moved slowly. Carth stumbled back from him, tripping over her feet in her attempt to get away.

In the sliver of moonlight, she could trace the dark lines running up his flesh, moving like ink tracing beneath his skin and racing toward his face. She had seen it before on the man in the street.

Felyn's eyes went wide.

"Release this!" he demanded. His voice was thready, but power radiated in the command. He stalked forward, and then staggered, reminding her of what had happened to the man who had attacked Kel.

Jhon caught Felyn's sword as it swung toward Carth. One hand clutched his side. "She has no control. There is only one release."

Felyn swung again, power pulsing from him, but Jhon caught it again. Felyn staggered and then fell to his knees.

The A'ras stepped forward. "We could learn much from him," she said to Jhon.

"We will learn nothing. The girl has strength, but no control."

Felyn dropped to the ground. His body trembled and thrashed. The blackness consumed his exposed skin, covering his face and hands.

"Some would consider his loss a shame," the A'ras said. Looking past Jhon and toward the hut, she shook her head. "I am not one of them."

Felyn stopped twitching.

As he did, shadows seeped away from him.

Carth could not see them, but she could feel them.

Had she somehow used the shadows to kill Felyn?

The A'ras woman turned to Carth. "You will have questions. Your parents were right in bringing you to us. There is much you can learn."

Carth shook her head, looking at Jhon. "I don't think I can."

"You can learn to control the flame. That is why they brought you here. That is how you stopped him," the A'ras said, looking down at Felyn.

The flame? Carth didn't understand. All she knew was that she was *not* blessed. Would someone blessed be able to use power to harm another? Would she be able to kill?

She looked away from Felyn and saw Etan standing near the shore with his shoulders slumped. As angry as he might be, he had cared about Kel. If nothing else, Carth knew that. But he had sided with the Thevers, and he should face punishment.

"I don't know what I am. He took my parents before I

could learn," Carth said. After everything that had happened to her, she knew she wasn't blessed. Not with her parents' death, and losing Stiv, and nearly losing Taryn. She had no blessings.

The A'ras touched her shoulder, her hand warm and her grip gentle. "You may be of Ih-lash, Ms. Rel, but you are also something more." She met Carth's eyes, holding her gaze a moment. "Your mother was right to bring you to us. If you would like, you may come and learn."

"Learn what?"

The A'ras smiled. "To control your power. To be more than what you are. To become one of the A'ras."

Cloaked in shadow, Carth stood outside the Wounded Lyre, listening to the steady rhythm of music coming from within. Etan had returned, and though Carth thought he deserved punishment for what he'd done, the A'ras did not want to draw any more attention to Felyn and the others like him. She could still hear Kel's excitement at seeing Taryn again. He wouldn't have felt the same for her, she didn't think. Through the windows of the tavern, she saw that Hal still lived, and her heart sung for that fact, but she couldn't enter, maybe not ever again.

"You look troubled."

She looked up, surprised by how quietly Jhon had appeared. There were more secrets to him than she understood, but those were answers she would learn in time.

"I… I'm losing another home."

Jhon nodded solemnly. "You were never meant for that home, Carth."

She swallowed the lump in her throat. "It seems I was never meant to have *any* home."

"Your parents brought you to Nyaesh for a reason."

She closed her eyes and sighed. "That's the problem. I have to take it on faith that they wanted me here, and that they wanted me to learn from the A'ras, when they never said anything about that. They never told me anything about why we came to Nyaesh."

"Ih-lash faded, Carth, and they could not remain. Have you never wondered why they wandered?"

"I never knew."

"The Hjan hunt those with power and claim those they can. The children they want. Many were born to the A'ras, or to Reshian, and they would use them. If that fails, they destroy the rest. So many of your father's people suffered."

"Only my father's?"

"I think your mother had a different heritage, or you would not have the potential to learn from the A'ras."

"They can't teach me about shadows, can they?" She hadn't seen any of the A'ras ever display anything like a shadow ability.

"Not the shadows—you must keep that to yourself for now—but they are a start."

"Only a start? What does that mean?"

"That means that it is a start," Jhon said. "You will learn more in time, but you must make the first move, and then there will be others." He smiled at her, and it transformed his face, this time making him seem much older. "I believe you are familiar with the order of things like that?"

Another game, only this time, her parents wouldn't be there to teach her.

She watched the tavern as the door opened. Kel stood in the doorway, searching the night, but he wouldn't be able to see her where she stood.

Her heart hammered and sadness gnawed at her stomach.

She could release the shadows and return to the tavern… but she would never learn what more she could do, or what she could be.

"I'm scared," she told Jhon.

He patted her on the shoulder, a gesture that reminded her in some ways of her father. "We are born to fear change because it hurts, but this change, I think, will lead you to something greater. When you are ready, I will take you to them."

Carth watched the tavern until Kel stepped back and closed the door. She sighed, releasing the shadows as she breathed out. What else could she do? She couldn't remain here and collect scraps, not when she knew she could be something more. Neither of her parents would have wanted that for her.

Pulling her gaze away from the tavern, she started along the street toward the palace, and the A'ras, and the first move in a new game.

END

Acknowledgements:

I want to thank all the people who helped me get this book together, including all my awesome beta readers, West of Mars editing, Clio Editing, Polgarus Studios for print formatting, my fantastic cover designer, and mostly, my family for allowing me the time to do the work!

About the Author:

New York Times and USA Today Bestselling Author D.K. Holmberg lives in Minnesota and is the author of multiple series including The Cloud Warrior Saga, The Dark Ability, The Endless War, and The Lost Garden. When he's not writing, he's chasing around his two active children.

Check my website for updates and new releases:
http://www.dkholmberg.com.

Follow me on Facebook:
www.facebook.com/dkholmberg

I'm occasionally on twitter:
www.twitter.com/dkholmberg

Also By DK Holmberg

59908188R00171

Made in the USA
San Bernardino, CA
07 December 2017